DANGEROUS WATERS

On holiday in the enchanting Hungarian village of Szentendre, schoolteacher Cassandra Sutherland meets handsome local artist Matthias Benedek, and soon both are swept up in a romance as dreamy as the moon on the Danube. But Matt is hiding secrets from Cass, and she is determined never to love another man like her late fiancé, whose knack for getting into dangerous situations was the ruin of them both. Can love conquer all once it's time for Cass to return home to London?

SHEILA DAGLISH

DANGEROUS WATERS

Complete and Unabridged

LINFORD
Leicester

First published in Great Britain in 2016

First Linford Edition
published 2017

A catalogue record for this book is available
from the British Library.

ISBN 978–1–4448–3255–6

Published by
F. A. Thorpe (Publishing)
Anstey, Leicestershire

Set by Words & Graphics Ltd.
Anstey, Leicestershire
Printed and bound in Great Britain by
T. J. International Ltd., Padstow, Cornwall

This book is printed on acid-free paper

1

He looks ill, thought Cassandra. Then, *No, he looks as though he's* been *ill*.

The man was thin, too thin, his olive skin so pale that the shadowy line of stubble lent him a villainous air, at odds with his smile. Dark hair, almost but not quite straight, brushed the collar of the sky-blue shirt which hung loosely on his frame. Cass had seen many Hungarians with brown, almost black, eyes, but his were the luminous blue-grey which she'd noticed in others.

Hurriedly she held out her hand so that he could count a few coins into her palm, the change from her purchase. A hint of amusement crossed his face, as though he was aware of her interest, but relieved that it held no predatory gleam.

Magda peered over Cass's shoulder. 'That's lovely! Is it your own work?' She glanced at him appraisingly. Cass hid a smile. That was the way Magda invariably looked at men.

The man nodded, even as he cast critical eyes over the small landscape painting that he was wrapping. Its colours were muted, predominantly shades of yellow and dull gold; the long, squat farmhouses with their thatched roofs bedded into the dusty ground as if, many moons ago, they had been planted there.

'Yes, thank you. I am glad you find it pleasing. I can show you others with a similar view, if you are interested.' It wasn't the usual salesman's pitch, merely a polite suggestion. He'd met many young women like this and wondered if he'd ever feel free to flirt with one — maybe this one — as he might have done a year ago. She was attractive, but too obvious. Her friend, on the other hand, looked content to remain a background figure, although she was by far the more interesting one. She stood almost within reach, but a sense of distance was there, a drift of gauze as impenetrable as a wall of steel.

Cass, unaware of his thoughts, looked away, feeling her smile deepen. Magda's appreciation of the painting was real, but even more genuine was her interest in the artist. The two friends had wandered up through the main street of Szentendre, a charming small town beside the River Danube. It was a tourists' paradise, with sunny streets, souvenir shops, and numerous bars and small restaurants, set amidst the picturesque architecture of Hungary. Before reaching the central square, a generous display of paintings had lured them through wrought-iron gates into a courtyard which was bordered on three sides by a single-storey house. Its walls were weathered, but their flaking ochre paintwork was almost hidden behind cascades of scarlet and pink bougainvillea. Elsewhere, geraniums, fragrant summer daisies and lilies spilled from window-boxes and from urns set haphazardly on every ledge around the building and enclosure.

Cass had fallen in love with the landscape, a framed canvas, which she bought.

It would look good above her desk at home, and remind her of this unexpected holiday. Experience warned that Magda was likely to take a while before deciding whether or not to buy, so she propped herself on the low drystone wall and waited.

The Hungarian woman began looking at other canvases as the man took them from a stack that had been propped nearby. He balanced a few in front of the metal gates and stood, head slightly tilted, watching her.

It was no hardship, thought Cass. Her friend was beautiful, with dark eyes and long, straight black hair which gleamed in the sun, and a wide white smile. The two women couldn't have been more different in appearance. Cass knew that she, too, was considered attractive, but with fair hair and pale skin. Her mouth curved as she remembered Bryn. He hadn't been the type to give a woman compliments, but on one rare occasion in his late teens, he'd told Cass that she 'knocked spots off' all the others! A shadow passed across her

4

face and her lips compressed as she tried to push away the memory.

'I love this one!' Magda exclaimed. 'Acres of sunflowers, turning their heads to smile at the sun.' She regarded the artist with raised eyebrows. This wasn't the work of an amateur. 'I think you must have taken your paints and brushes to the Great Plain. There is such a wonderful sense of space.'

Cass also studied him with fresh interest. Lines radiating from beside his eyes betrayed experience of the world and, doubtless, of women. Cass suspected that he knew very well that Magda was sizing him up as a possible conquest, but his answer was courteous.

'Yes, I find the Plain awe-inspiring, quite magnificent. It is always difficult to leave there.' Cass had seen photographs of the vast sun-bleached Hortobágy, where rambling homesteads crouched beneath straw roofs; where long-horned cattle roamed, guarded by horsemen wearing black broad-brimmed hats; and where tall skeletal cross-beams marked

5

each life-giving well. He'd captured the essence of the land as she'd imagined it, and she longed to go there. If time allowed, perhaps a brief visit might be possible.

His gaze returned to Cass. Reluctant to be drawn into the conversation, she turned her head slightly to look beyond the gates into the street. On the corner, a pony and trap waited. Their owner wore a jaunty felt hat which probably reflected his optimism for a good day's trading. The street was busy, the slope gentle, the sky sunny, so he shouldn't have to wait long for a client or two.

'Are you spending a holiday in Szentendre? Or are you here for a few hours only?' the artist pointedly addressed Cass. He spoke perfect English, but with an accent that betrayed his origin.

Her reply was deliberately vague. 'We're here for a couple of days.' She didn't give any more information. He seemed decent enough, but it was Magda who would decide whether or not to encourage him. As for herself, Cass had no desire to become involved with a man — any man.

Magda, however, had cast a shrewd look at his face, but all his attention was concentrated on Cass. With a small sigh, she said, 'We have been staying with my parents in Budapest this past week. But they still keep our old home here in Szentendre, so I thought my friend would enjoy a few days away from the big-city dust and noise.'

Asking him to set aside the sunflower painting, she promised to return soon if she decided to buy it. Then, indicating an open square higher up the street where trestle benches were being set in place opposite a timbered stage, she asked, 'What is going to happen there?'

He followed her gaze. 'Tomorrow night there will be a musical performance. The orchestra will probably play light classics, as well as popular pieces from shows, and there will be singers.' Indicating a noticeboard a few metres away, he added, 'As a one-time resident, you will already know that a variety of entertainment is staged during the main tourist season. The music concerts are very popular. If you have time to spare, it's a pleasant way to spend an evening.'

He made the suggestion casually, despite wanting to encourage them, to see more of the quiet fair-haired woman, but knew he must let them go. This was no time for personal involvements. In any case, he sensed that she would resist any such overtures. As they said goodbye, he watched her walk away, with a sense of regret which he tried to put at the back of his mind.

Leaving him, the two young women explored the dusty, sun-dappled streets for a couple of hours, eventually stopping for drinks at a pavement café that overlooked the river. Cass said she would wait alone when Magda decided to return to the courtyard and buy the sunflower scene. The day was comfortably warm rather than hot, but with fair skin that burnt easily, she was glad of the striped sunshade. Despite his reserve, she was conscious that the artist had looked at her with particular interest, and that her friend had noticed.

'Are you sure you won't come with me? I'll leave the coast clear, if you wish!' Magda drained her glass of lemonade and rose from her chair. 'Although perhaps he was simply assessing your commercial value.'

'What are you talking about?' Cass said with a smile.

'He might want to paint you.' Magda hesitated. 'Nothing more.'

Cass's laughter rippled. Two tanned backpackers at the next table twisted their heads and grinned. Magda gave them a slight smile but then turned to leave. 'I shan't be long,' she said.

Cass watched her easy stride as she walked away, and thought how fortunate she was to have her as a friend. They had met nearly three years ago, when Magda came to England to teach at a local college. She had moved into a flat in the same building as Cass, who taught history at the nearby secondary school. It was a time when Cass was particularly in need of a new friend, someone who had no emotional involvement with the horror that still lingered every waking moment, changing her life forever.

Both were now twenty-five. When Magda realised that Cass had made no holiday plans, she was insistent: 'Come home with me! As a historian you will love Hungary! When you return to England, you can tell the children tales of Mongolian horsemen and St. Stephen's crown with its mysterious crooked cross. There's Matthias Corvinus, too, the Renaissance king. A fascinating man. I think you would call him the last of the big spenders, but a shrewd guy, all the same!'

Cass couldn't resist, and had been welcomed by Magda's parents, who, whilst retaining their family home in Szentendre, an hour's drive from the city, often found it more convenient to stay in their town flat, a short tram ride from the centre of Budapest. In a few years' time they would retire from the university where Magda's father, Professor Frankel, taught English literature and her mother, an older version of her daughter but without her offspring's lively, sometimes exhausting personality, was a philosopher. They were wonderful guides who were delighted to watch Cass succumb to the wide bustling streets, the timeless enchantment of the ancient Castle District with its imposing colour-washed buildings, and the river traffic as it passed beneath the Danube bridges. One evening they took her to a high point overlooking the water, a night that sparkled with the stars above, whilst below, a glittering carpet of lights turned the embankment into fairyland.

The four-storey mansion in Budapest was nowadays divided into apartments, and bore the wear and tear of years. It fascinated Cass. Behind the massive front door with its antique knocker, a wide staircase rose to the upper levels. In the entrance hall, faded paintwork etched a border of leaves in sage green and dull maroon. Upstairs, in the high-ceilinged apartment, dusty chandeliers hung low, almost touching the tall central-opening doors. Cass felt she wouldn't have been surprised to see a ghostly Mozart fling them open and seat himself at Magda's beloved piano. She was looking forward to spending more time there, after her few days in Szentendre.

When Magda returned to the café, carrying her new painting, Cass paid the waitress and they returned to the Frankels' cream-washed house, where earlier they had left their travel bags. Despite being unoccupied quite often, a local woman regularly came to open the windows and clear the inevitable dust before the family arrived, so its friendly welcome was always waiting for them.

Later, a few minutes' walk took the friends to a quiet street where Magda's cousin, Sophie, lived with her husband. Cass quickly felt as though she had known them for years. Slightly older than Magda, Sophie was tall and well-built, with warm brown eyes and an appealing smile. Her husband, Laszlo, appeared an amiable man, happy to remain a quiet background figure. He worked for a local ferry company, and Sophie was happy with her job in a small nursery school.

They chatted for a while before she suggested an inexpensive restaurant which Magda also knew and liked. Laughingly, Cass insisted that she wanted to order a dish that was completely Hungarian — 'with not a hint of English roast beef or sausage and chips!' The others were happy to study the menu, and eventually decided on a delicious meal of veal with roasted peppers, and a bottle of golden Tokay wine.

Sophie described her work at the school and told them how she and Laszlo hoped one day to start a family. 'But first we must earn enough money to buy a house. It need not be large, but our apartment is far too small, and without a garden of course.'

After their meal, she made her apologies. 'My head is like a sieve,' she said ruefully, and Magda nodded agreement with the cheeky familiarity of a close cousin as Sophie, pushing back her chair, admitted that she had forgotten to prepare papers for a staff meeting tomorrow. 'It is quite an important one because we shall be choosing applicants to interview for an unexpected vacancy. One of our younger helpers has to leave because her mother is seriously ill, so Bori must go home to Balaton.' Bestowing an airy kiss towards both Magda and Cass, she hurried away, leaving them to wander to a vantage point overlooking the Danube.

In an open space encircled by trees, a few market people were packing up their trestle tables. Cass stopped to admire an ecru table runner worked in fine linen. The stallholder, a stout middle-aged woman, was keen to demonstrate how she had done the intricate embroidery. It would make a good present for her father and his new wife, decided Cass. And she needed to make extra effort to welcome Liz. The advent of a stepmother not much older than herself had been the final desolate step.

'Look! Isn't that the artist?' Magda indicated a man who was leaning against the low parapet, his profile etched sharply against the dusky pink horizon. 'He interests me — although it's *you* that interests *him*.' She looked at Cass. Her friend's profile, like the artist's, was outlined against the sky: delicate bones, a small straight nose, and a mouth that was habitually held in a straight line.

Cass glanced at him, and then her eyes moved to the young woman at his side. 'Yes, and there's his wife.'

Magda made a moue of disappointment and suggested that before returning home, they should stop on the way for a final coffee. 'Our artist might have a wife, but I still think he was interested in you, Cassandra Sutherland,' she persisted as they sat watching people stroll in the warm evening air.

Cass decided to ignore her. 'You've got a moustache of froth.'

Magda brushed it away with the back of her hand. 'If you had been more friendly, he might have wanted to paint you. And then you would have been immortalised.'

Cass chuckled. 'Did I ever tell you that you're ridiculous? Anyway, there wouldn't be time.'

Magda sighed and leant to touch her hand. 'I don't mean to pester you, my friend. But life is short. I wish that you could move on and be happy.'

'I'm quite content.' Cass squeezed Magda's fingers affectionately, knowing her companion didn't mean to be hurtful. 'I've learnt to accept the fact that Bryn has gone. I sometimes wonder if it'd been better if we'd had at least a few months of marriage. To lose him just days before the wedding was devastating.' Her lips quivered as she struggled for control. The emptiness never left her.

'And then, of course, you lost his mother.' After Bryn's death, his widowed mother had been persuaded to visit her sister, who lived in Australia. The holiday had been extended, and then extended again. As active as her son had been, she was helping her sister run a small restaurant, and it seemed likely that she would settle there permanently. Her departure had been unexpected and something that saddened Cass, although she had been genuinely encouraging. But it meant the almost inevitable loss of a staunch and affectionate friend.

Cass's laugh was hollow. 'And after that, to all intents and purposes, my father went wandering too!' She didn't need to explain that after her mother died, ten-year-old Cass had been brought up by her father and a succession of housekeepers. Life would have been lonely had it not been for their neighbour, Mrs. Weston and her son, Bryn. Despite very different personalities, the children had been inseparable throughout their childhood and teenage years. Cass couldn't remember Bryn asking her to marry him unless it was the day she'd strapped up his ankle after a rock-climbing accident.

'We'll buy a house with a workshop once we're married. I'll need one for all my gear.' He'd grinned. 'Including an outsize first-aid kit!'

Cass shuddered, remembering where Bryn's adventurous spirit had led. To make matters worse, a year ago Peter Sutherland, her father, fell in love with

Liz Thomas, fifteen years his junior. At first, Cass was appalled by their plan to marry, but found that she couldn't help liking Liz. The only trouble was that, despite the welcome she always received when visiting them, Cass suddenly felt distanced from her father, with whom she had once been so close. It seemed as though everyone had gone, leaving her behind.

Magda decided it was wise to leave the subject, for the moment, at least. Instead she suggested that they might enjoy the open-air performance tomorrow night.

'And then we shall have wonderful music in our heads when we return to England to mark exercise books with big black crosses!'

Laughing, Cass agreed.

2

The following evening, she sat with Magda on the tiers of wooden benches that had been erected in the centre of Szentendre. The air was balmy, the crowded audience in high spirits and the music enjoyable, mainly popular classics played by a visiting orchestra. A choir of about twenty women wearing traditional costume accompanied talented soloists, and the cleverly chosen repertoire included songs from stage shows, which suited everyone, whatever their age or taste.

As they made their way out at the end of the performance, Magda nudged Cass and indicated a thin dark-haired man standing on the bottom step of the gangway. It was the artist. He was steadying his wife, a slender brunette, as she descended, and then he took the hand of the fair-haired girl, aged about six, who came closely behind her. *The complete family group,* thought Cass with a pang. Would she and Bryn have been parents by now? She banished the shadows as Magda caught her arm and drew her unwillingly towards the trio.

'Hello again!' Magda greeted him with her usual friendly charm. 'We must thank you for recommending the concert. It was lovely.'

'I am glad you enjoyed it. Even this little one sat still, from beginning to end.' He flicked the blue ribbon securing the child's ponytail and then turned to the woman beside him. 'May I introduce my good friend, Anna?' His lips quirked as he cast her a sidelong glance. 'She and her husband are good enough to employ me — my official title is 'resident dauber of canvas'.' He drew the little girl forward. 'And this is my god-daughter, Lili. Say good evening in your very best English, please.'

Lili obliged, with a shy smile.

With a slight bow that mirrored the attractive accent and betrayed his European roots, he said, 'And I am Matthias Benedek.' Tonight the shadowy stubble had gone, and the taut, smooth lines of his jaw, together with high cheekbones and strongly marked black eyebrows, turned him into a man who would always stand out in a crowd.

Magda's relief at his bachelor status had been obvious to Cass, although with a tinge of irritation she wished her friend would leave well alone. As he looked at them enquiringly, Magda hurried to cover her silence.

'I'm glad you have found time to relax away from your canvases.' She glanced at Cass and, finding no response, carried on regardless. 'I am Magda Frankel. Hungary is my homeland, of course, but my friend is thoroughly English.' Her smile was mischievous. 'Although her given name comes from ancient Greece.'

'And that is?' His eyes were intent.

'I'm Cassandra Sutherland.' Cass remained casual, despite a flicker of uncertainty. For some reason, this stranger unsettled her normal calm.

'Forgive me for being personal, but it's a big name for a not very large lady!' His charming lopsided grin made it a compliment.

Cass conceded that she *was* a bit short, compared with his friend, Anna. She'd often found her lack of height a trial, especially years ago at school, when it came to scoring goals on the netball pitch. Even wearing high heels, she would only reach his shoulder. His gaze seemed riveted on the delicate oval of her face. The reason soon became clear as he noticed her expression register discomfort.

'Forgive me for staring,' he said. 'At the concert I pointed you out to Anna and she agreed that you would be a splendid subject for a portrait. Is there a chance that you would agree to sit for me?'

Cass shook her head. 'I'm sorry, Mr. Benedek. We shall only be here for a few days. But thank you for even considering me. I'm honoured.' Her eyes suddenly danced. 'Unless you plan to use me in a painting of Dracula's wife — after all, we're not far from Transylvania!'

His face had stilled when she broke into laughter. Now he also laughed. 'No, I assure you! I have no interest in vampires!'

Before Cass realised it, they were all sitting around a table in a quieter street leading from the centre, and Matthias Benedek was ordering drinks. She didn't know who had made the suggestion, but suspected that it was Magda. Or perhaps it had been Matthias, hoping by subtle persuasion to wear her down until she agreed to act as his model!

Anna explained that she and her husband had been friends with Matthias since their schooldays. Her husband worked for a small commercial airline, so was often away, piloting groups of tourists or business people to other areas of Hungary, or even further afield. 'So I am glad of Matt's company this summer, even though he sells more of his own paintings than he does mine!'

'You live elsewhere?' Magda asked him directly.

He hesitated. 'Yes, but I have been ill, and my friends insisted that I stay with them for a while.' He volunteered no more information, and Cass noticed the swift glance he shot Anna when she began to speak.

The Hungarian woman hurriedly changed whatever she had been about to say, asking instead: 'Tell us what you think of my town, and for how long you stay in Hungary.'

Magda explained that she had been born in Szentendre but later went to college in Budapest. At the end of a teacher-training course, she had applied for and obtained a job at a language college in England. 'But this is Cassandra's first trip to Hungary,' she said.

'You also teach?' The question came from Matthias. It wasn't just a polite question, but an undisguised wish to know more about her. Berating himself for this unwise emotion, he told himself that there was no harm in encouraging her to disclose more of herself. It took little perception to realise that her real 'self' was enclosed by an invisible stake fence. She quickly rewarded his curiosity.

'Yes. I love it.' Imperceptibly, Cass found herself opening to his quiet, genuine interest.

'And what subject do you teach?'

'History.' She knew this wouldn't be the last of his questions.

'An interesting discipline,' he commented, hoping she might reveal even more if he could keep her talking. 'You obviously have a good memory.'

'Or simply an obsession with the past!' Cass retorted, inexplicably pleased when his lean face creased with appreciative amusement.

Time passed swiftly as Magda recounted anecdotes of a teacher's life in England, although she admitted to embellishing a few of her more outrageous tales.

'A class of teenage boys and girls must be a daunting experience at times.' Matthias looked at Cass, deliberately drawing her back into the conversation, noting how she was content to let her friend enjoy the limelight. 'Do you find it difficult to interest them in long-ago events?' His gaze appreciated the way fine beams from a string of white fairy lights played on Cass's hair which, short and feather-cut, flicked upwards to form a pale gold halo around her small head. Wide and clear, her grey eyes were invariably serious, so that when she was amused, they lit in a way which he found intensely appealing.

She frowned, considering. 'One hurdle is persuading children to look beyond the fact that Henry VIII had six wives. The kids chant an aide-memoire: 'Divorced, beheaded, died; divorced, beheaded, survived'. Their faces go blank when you point out Henry's military aspirations and the religious turmoil he caused. They only wake up again when the syllabus moves on to Bloody Mary!' An unaccountable warmth crept into her veins as she spotted the twinkle in his eye, as though they were sharing a private joke. Unconsciously, she relaxed.

They learnt little in turn about Matthias Benedek. Adeptly he side-stepped any attempt to discover more. He was undoubtedly talented, perhaps even famous. Maybe he was enjoying a period of anonymity whilst recovering from his illness. When Magda asked about it, he said it was a bacterial infection that had struck him down when he was abroad.

'Abroad?'

A brief look — could it have been annoyance? — flashed across his features. 'Africa,' he said, but didn't enlarge, and smoothly guided conversation into other channels.

It had been an enjoyable interlude, thought Cass later that night as she relaxed in her comfortable bedroom. Leaning back against her pillows, she sighed. Matthias was an attractive man, and she was honest enough to acknowledge that quite apart from his physical appeal, he was someone she would like to spend more time with. It needn't involve commitment, she told herself; just casual friendship. She had allowed herself to become so traumatised that to be a normal, laughing, even loving woman had seemed unthinkable. And an artist would be safe.

27

If they met again, perhaps she should allow herself to enjoy his company.

Yawning, she slid beneath the lightweight cover. She would probably never see him again.

* * *

Sophie's husband, Laszlo, had suggested that Cass and Magda should take a journey by boat along the Danube. It sounded the perfect way to spend a day, so after breakfast the next morning they packed a few sandwiches and walked to the ferry terminal.

Magda hadn't been on the river since childhood, but remembered taking a cruise that had followed a particularly scenic route upstream. Cass was happy to fall in with her suggestion. Glancing at her watch, Magda frowned slightly.

'Our boat won't leave for another hour. We might as well sit where we can watch the river traffic.' Already, below them, a cluster of six small craft, probably members of a yacht club, were skimming the

28

ripples as their sails captured the light breeze. At this early hour there were few visitors about. Later in the day the pavements would be alive with holiday-makers, and tourist-packed steamers would give the Danube its summer carnival air.

Local people used the river transport too, coming and going between regular stopping-points both down and upstream. Someone was waiting now, a young woman with a heavy shopping basket and a screaming child. The toddler had fallen and grazed her knee, and wasn't in a mood to be easily pacified. Her brother, a curly-headed five-year-old, took advantage while the mother's back was turned. Drawn to the water as a bear to honey, he pulled himself up onto the embankment wall. Precariously scrambling to his feet, he laughed and waved as an early plea-sure boat approached the wharf. A crystal ball wasn't necessary. One wobble was all it took. Falling, he hit the jetty too fast to grab the edge and safety. The ship's siren blasted; the crew shouted; a woman screamed. Just one slight splash came as the water closed over the boy's head.

Cass was already on her feet and running. But the man who had been leaning against green metal railings with sketch-pad and pen was faster. Leaping onto the wall, his body arched as he dived into the water. The steamer was juddering to a reluctant halt, its crew flinging lifebelts over the side. In seconds both the man and boy would be crushed to death. Reaching out for the child, with desperate strength the swimmer dragged him clear.

Drawn by the commotion, onlookers rushed to haul them from the river. The boy was hysterical, his mother alternately shouting and comforting. For one brief moment, everyone's attention was on the little family.

Quietly, his rescuer began to walk away. Cass watched as he pushed back the dark hair that was plastered to his skull. Already she'd recognised him. Matthias Benedek.

A young man, camera strapped to his shoulder, was chasing after him. Blocking

Matthias's path, he started shooting questions. What was his name? Where did he live? Was he on holiday, or just a day-tripper? Matthias, clothes saturated, shook his head impatiently. The questioner hurried beside him, persistence labelling him a journalist, keen to sell story and photograph.

'Fritz Ramm,' Matthias flung at last, and added in German, '*Ein Ausflügler aus Hamburg.*' Quickly he lifted one hand to his face as the camera snapped. '*Jetzt lassen Sie mich allein!*' With long, impatient strides, he brushed his tormentor aside and was gone.

Cass knew enough of the language to understand what he had said: 'Fritz Ramm, a day-tripper from Hamburg. Now leave me alone!'

Magda also heard. 'The strong, silent type. An undercover hero!'

Cass nodded. 'He's got pretty good reflexes. I'd swear he only noticed the boy when he saw me running.'

Magda assessed her friend's white T-shirt and red cropped trousers. 'Well,

I am glad he got there first. You look good today. Neat and sweet. It would be a shame to soak your outfit in dirty river water!'

Cass obliged with a theatrical shudder, but then found that she couldn't laugh. Nor could she control her shaking limbs. A flash of memory had taken her to another day, another river.

Magda, always sensitive, realised. She took hold of Cass's arm. 'Come on! We've just time for a nice restorative coffee before we set sail.'

There was no sign of Matthias. Swiftly he'd left the embankment, ignoring curious eyes as, garments sodden, he headed for home. Cursing silently, he knew he'd had a narrow escape. A photograph, even for a local newspaper, was dangerous, and the dramatic rescue might even have reached the national press. Until Paul recovered, he must avoid being noticed ... as long as Paul *did* recover!

★   ★   ★

The voyage on a spacious white steamer lasted several hours, allowing Cass and Magda to enjoy the scenery and the gentle, gleaming swell. Seagulls swooped low, following the frothy trail along the Danube. Other passengers, many Hungarian but some Dutch or German, leant back on slatted wooden seats, revelling in the warmth of a cloudless blue sky.

Magda nudged Cass. 'Methinks the lady hath enjoyed the sun a little too much!' She grinned. 'My apologies to your wonderful Shakespeare!'

Cass looked to where a plump woman had pulled her skirt up above chubby knees. She had moved the straps of her sundress to reveal white stripes, stark against the raw red of previous sunburn. 'Ouch!' She shuddered. 'That must be a souvenir from yesterday. How can she take such a risk again?' When Cass was a child, she'd suffered an overdose of sun and vowed never to repeat the experience. 'I've an urge to take her my sun lotion and tell her to cover up.'

'She'd probably rap you around the

ears with it!'

As they disembarked a few hours later, Magda remembered that she had promised to call at the pharmacy to collect a prescription for Sophie, who occasionally suffered migraines and had been grateful for her cousin's offer.

'There is no need for you to come unless you feel energetic.' Indicating a street which sloped gently uphill, Magda added, 'Why not take another look at Anna's studio?' She didn't mention Matthias. 'I'll meet you at the vendéglö on the corner by the river and we can have a snack there, or just a coffee.'

Cass agreed. Much as she enjoyed her friend's company, it would be good to wander alone. As for Matthias and his paintings, well, perhaps she'd go, perhaps not. Firstly, though, she wanted to take a look at the cemetery, which occupied a quiet area she hadn't yet explored. But when she reached the site where rows of white marble headstones stood, her footsteps slowed.

A number of people were there, putting

fresh flowers in the black-lettered urns, or cleaning the marble. Most of them were women, some quite elderly. One family group caught her attention. Quickly she retreated, not wanting to be seen.

It was Matthias. With him was Anna. Between them, holding their hands, stood Lili. They did not speak, and their faces were serious.

Cass edged away and walked carefully along a path that was separated from them by a cluster of trees and neatly tended shrubbery. When Cass reached the end and glanced over her shoulder, they had gone. Making sure firstly that there was no sign of them in the quiet enclosure, curiosity drew her back to look at the memorial they had been facing. She thought it might be the grave of Anna's parents. But no, it was the resting place of a man, Stephen Lendvag, who had died at the age of twenty-four. Who was he? Cass wondered.

She didn't follow Magda's suggestion to visit the studio courtyard, though Matthias and Anna had said they would be welcome at any time. She had a feeling that Matthias wouldn't want to refer to the episode on the quayside. Moreover, after seeing the little group in the cemetery, Cass felt that today she would be intruding. Their attitude had been sombre, one of love and respect, and of grief that still lingered.

Her mobile phone rang. It was Magda. She had unexpectedly come across some people who used to be her neighbours. They were insistent that she must join them for a late lunch, but the discussion was likely to centre on mutual friends, which would be boring for Cass. Would Cass mind eating alone?

Lunch alone in this lovely town was no hardship, she decided, and chose a restaurant where small tables were dotted on a tree-shaded patio. The waitress came after a few minutes, a friendly teenager who recommended a meat dish spiced with peppers and served with tiny dumplings. Hopefully the portions would be small; if not, then tonight a salad would be all she could manage. The girl moved away to take another order. A tall figure took her place.

'Matthias!' An unexpected surge of pleasure lifted Cass's voice. She wasn't to know that the brightness in her grey eyes and an involuntary smile reassured the man, who had wondered about his welcome.

'Matt, please. That is what my friends call me.' He indicated a chair. 'You will allow me to join you? Or will your companion object?'

'Magda? No, she's lunching with some old acquaintances.' Cass knew she was revealing too much pleasure. Avoiding any reference to what she'd seen in the cemetery, innocently asked: 'Is business slack today?'

He shook his head. 'Not particularly. But I must eat!' Lowering his voice, he confided mock-seriously, 'I still have a schoolboy craving for hot dogs, but then I saw you and hoped you would agree to share a grown-up meal with me.'

Cass tried to hide her feelings behind a noncommittal smile. Suddenly the day had taken on an extra brightness, an almost-forgotten sense of anticipation.

Quickly, as though fearing that she would retreat into her shell, Matt asked, 'Have you read much of the history of my country?'

Secretly amused by his blatant choice of a subject likely to interest her, Cass shook her head. 'Not as much as I wanted before my holiday. Magda's invitation came at a busy time of the term, when I was marking exam papers till midnight.' She waited while he placed his order with the waitress. 'I was intrigued by the little I managed to read about one of your kings, Matthias Corvinus. Are you named after him?'

'Assuredly! I like to think I have his love of art and literature, all those things that he brought to Hungary.'

'I suppose you'd call him a Renaissance man, the first in eastern Europe?'

'Yes; he brought Italian artists, poets, and artisans to this country, but he was wise enough to maintain the old traditions. The nobles were unhappy with the changes he introduced, so he was careful to reassure them that certain things would remain the same.' Seeing that Cass's interest was genuine, he asked, 'Have you visited his summer palace at Visegrád? It is not far from here.' As she shook her head, he added, 'It is mainly in ruins, of course, but there are still remains of the past.'

They lingered over their food, and their conversation ranged across many areas where they shared a mutual interest. She liked to watch the way the corner of Matthias's mouth lifted to deepen the creases in his lean cheeks, and she liked his eyes — were they more grey or more blue? Their crystal-clear shade intrigued her. Today, again, he wore an open-necked blue shirt and light canvas slacks, but there was more colour in his cheeks, and the look of exhaustion from their first meeting had faded. There was no comparison with the river-drenched man from early morning.

'I have no wish to intrude, but I must ask ... ' His long, artistic fingers toyed with the handle of a spoon as he paused momentarily, before lifting his head to meet her gaze. 'You are a beautiful woman, and yet you do not wear a ring. Why has no man captured you by now?' His voice held more than curiosity; it held a depth of interest which warned that he wanted an answer. Aware that opening the gates to personal issues was foolish, even unsafe, he still couldn't resist a growing need to know more about this quietly captivating Englishwoman. In many ways she seemed fresh and untouched, and yet a depth of experience and loss was there in her clear grey eyes.

Cass drew a deep breath. Even after three years, she found it difficult to put into words. She could politely tell him to mind his own business, or she could make some flippant reply that warned him off the subject. On the other hand, she'd realised that on the rare occasions when she'd been obliged to describe what had happened, the events of that terrible day became easier to accept. It wasn't that she'd ever get over it, but slowly she was becoming used to it.

Her fingers traced a pattern on the red tablecloth as she looked down, seeing nothing. How could she find the words? But his listening silence told her there was no need for haste. 'I was engaged to be married. Bryn died in an accident a few days before our wedding.'

Matthias's hand reached across the table to cover hers. 'I am sorry. Can you bear to tell me — what sort of accident?'

Her face was bleak. Matt knew she had travelled far away from him, to a place that held tragedy. The background murmur of voices from other tables faded, the occasional burst of laughter no more than a distant echo, the waitress serving steaming dishes of food no more than a shadow.

'I'd known him all my life.' Cass lifted shadowed eyes, but then earlier memories tilted her mouth in a half-smile. 'Bryn had always been a sport-loving, outdoors type of boy. When an aunt bequeathed him some money, he set up an outdoor adventure company with two friends.

41

They revelled in every activity you can think of — water sports, rock-climbing, abseiling, cycling — you name it, Bryn did it!'

'Something went wrong.' It was not a question; more a statement.

Cass nodded, her smile vanishing. The contours of her face changed, making her look older than her years. 'He took a group of teenagers out in kayaks. There was quite a swell on the river that day, but it added to the fun, and most of them were experienced. It should've been safe enough.' Her expression darkened and her voice dropped almost to a whisper. 'One of the newer members started acting the fool. A stupid, crazy thing to do! Anyway, his kayak overturned. Somehow it caught between some rocks. We could see he was hurt and couldn't open the spray deck. Bryn dived in and managed to release him.' Digging her teeth into her lower lip, she tried to control her voice, hardly aware that Matt, leaning forward again, had captured her other hand also.

'Tell me,' he urged softly. His grasp was

strong, firm, comforting.

'There were tree roots, long and tough, like steel ropes. Bryn became hopelessly entangled. We couldn't cut him free. He drowned.' Her eyes were wet and he knew she was reliving a scene from hell. 'I'd gone to watch, though I'd never shared his love for water sports. I skidded down the bank and was there in the river beside him. But we couldn't save him.'

'And you have never been free of the nightmare.'

Wordlessly, she shook her head.

Releasing her hands, he poured a glass of wine and held it to her lips. 'Drink.'

Obediently she sipped, and then took the glass from him, savouring the warmth as she swallowed. He didn't ask any more, but skilfully, she realised later, eased their talk into less emotive channels. Afterwards they walked slowly to the studio courtyard, where a few prospective customers were admiring paintings. Anna was busy serving a stout Dutch tourist, but winked at Cass and mimed a drink of something cool.

Cass was tempted to stay; it was seductively relaxing to be here amidst the artwork and flowers. A tiny voice whispered that even if Matt was busy talking to prospective buyers, she wanted to sit quietly and watch him. There was a calm strength about him that appealed to her very much. She couldn't help comparing it with Bryn's ebullient nature, his extravagant gestures and quicksilver change of mood. Because she had been accustomed to them, she'd learned to accept them. With a slight frown, she wondered for the first time if she had merged into the background, his adoring follower. It was hard not to contrast that shadowy disciple with the Cassandra whom Matt had drawn out to talk about her work and opinions on so many different subjects.

The tranquillity of the scene was only broken once when Anna called to Matt that there was a telephone call for him. 'It is a business matter,' she explained to Cass.

Cass wondered why Matt needed to take the call, since the art shop was, in fact, Anna's. Her curiosity was aroused still more when he returned. Something had obviously displeased him. His brow was furrowed and his mouth grim. It was the first time that she had seen him so; they hadn't known each other long, but his normal manner seemed relaxed and easy-going.

Seeing her enquiring eyes, he shook off whatever was troubling him and merely said, 'An irritating little problem. It is nothing to worry about.' Bending over a stack of watercolours, he asked lightly, 'Have you sold any paintings in my absence?' He obviously didn't want to say more, so Cass followed his lead and admitted with a doleful face that she had sold none at all. Anna had gone indoors, returning soon with a tray that held tall frosted glasses of fruit juice. Once she had finished hers, Cass stood, ready to go.

Matt walked with her. To her surprise, as they wandered down the main street, still busy in the afternoon sun, he suggested that she might enjoy a drive to the summer palace of Matthias Corvinus. She wasn't to know that as soon as the words left his mouth, he was cursing himself for being a fool. It was too late to draw them back.

'Your friend would be welcome, of course, but I think you, particularly, might be intrigued by its history.' Ruefully he added, 'There's plenty of that, but very few walls!'

When they reached Magda's home, Matt said a brief goodbye, agreeing to return in an hour. Then he took her hand in his and gently touched the open palm with his lips. As she watched him leave, Cass's fingers curled, as though to keep hold of the kiss. She could almost hear the gates of her heart as they opened a fraction.

Surprised and pleased when Cass suggested the outing, Magda discreetly kept her thoughts to herself as she refused Matt's invitation. She had other plans. 'My friends' son, Zoltan, joined us for lunch. I knew him years ago when we were younger — but, oh, how he's grown!' Expressively, she rolled her dark eyes.

Cass chuckled. The Hungarian woman was incorrigible. She gave every appearance of being a man-eater, but when it came to going out on a date, was surprisingly selective. Once or twice she'd seemed smitten, but only for a while, and remained resolutely heart-whole. It looked as though Cass would have Matt to herself for the day.

3

The drive to Visegrád was full of interest, not only because of the scenery, but also because Matt was such good company. He'd warned Cass to bring a scarf to wear in his green open-topped car, and she was conscious that as she tied it, his eyes were appreciating the mixture of blue silk, sunshine and soft gold hair. She was beginning to like his attention, she realised, especially since he made no demands in return. But what if he did? Not knowing the answer, she pushed the thought away. As they drove, occasionally they fell silent, but it was a comfortable silence.

Reaching the site of the summer palace, they purchased a guide book, although Matt was familiar with the layout. 'You can add it to the pile of brochures and maps I am sure you have already bought,' he commented with a sideways smile that grew broader as she admitted, somewhat defensively, that her suitcase would be hard to close.

'You can see I did not exaggerate when I told you the palace was mainly ruins, but there's still a lingering atmosphere of the grandeur that was once here.' He was right — the tumbled walls were massive, their great stone blocks embedded in neatly trimmed grass. It took little to imagine the masonry towering to its original height, and mentally to clad the walls with precious tapestries, coloured banners, heraldic shields and crossed lances.

'Why don't you tell me what you know about its past?' suggested Cass. 'The problem with guide books is that you really need to read them before you reach the place you want to visit. Once you've explored, you find them more interesting because you've actually seen what they're describing.' Ruefully she added, 'And then, of course, you need to go back again.'

The fine lines beside his eyes deepened as he agreed. Since the sun was

49

particularly hot, they walked slowly, stopping frequently in shady spots. Cass often wore lightweight suits when she was teaching, but today was glad to be clad in a simple shift dress with cap sleeves. White, with sprigs of blue flowers and a simple tie-belt, it looked fresh and cool. When Matt said as much, she screwed up her nose.

'Thank you. But it's an optical illusion, I'm afraid! If I stayed long in the heat, I should melt!'

His low chuckle was sympathetic. He, too, was dressed for the weather in lightweight slacks and white shirt. His sunglasses didn't conceal his relaxed expression, nor did they hide his pleasure in her company.

Cass was certain that he had noticed her, and seen that she was racing to dive, before he had rescued the child from the river. But he was obviously loth to refer to his role in preventing a tragedy that would have shattered a family's world. Respecting his reticence, she made no mention of it, despite wondering at his aversion, even anger, when the journalist had tried to take a photograph. A 'happy snap' in the local news would surely not have mattered?

In fact, she suddenly realised that although they'd talked about so many things, she still knew nothing of his personal life. All she had learnt was that he'd been at school with Anna and her husband and that he currently worked in their art studio. Tempted to find out more, she remained silent. When, and if, he chose to tell her more was for Matt to decide. She wouldn't pry.

Drawing a long breath, she savoured the air, scented with the perfume of dried grasses and wild herbs. There was the indefinable aroma which comes from centuries-old fallen walls, rooted in tussocks of grass and mud-baked earth. It was a long time since she'd felt so at ease in a man's company; there was subtle enticement here. Did she want to enter this unknown world? The decision was up to her. Although Bryn was a beloved memory, he'd be the last person to hold her back from getting on with life.

She couldn't have dreamed of the conflict that was tearing at Matt's sense of sanity and reason as he strolled beside her. He knew that for months to come, he must offer nothing more than friendship, but his treacherous heart made every light touch a caress. As they reached the top of a worn, steep flight of steps, he caught her elbow and led her to a wooden bench.

'Rest! I cannot promise you a cool breeze, but at least we have some shade.'

As they sat in silence for a few minutes, Cass found her thoughts wandering in unfamiliar territory. What would it be like to kiss him? An involuntary glance at his mouth told her that it would be firm and warm and hard. Her pulse jumped. *You've heard too many schoolgirls spend their break-time talking about boys,* she scolded herself.

Seeing the sudden tilt of her lips, Matt asked: 'What's the joke?'

'I was thinking this is the ideal place for a history lesson,' she evaded. 'There's nothing like the on-site atmosphere to help you understand the past.'

'I imagine that Hungary occupies a very small space, if any, in your syllabus.'

'I'm afraid so! The curriculum is so jam-packed that we can only skim across your kings or queens, if at all.'

Holding out a hand after another spell of silence, he pulled Cass to her feet. 'It is time for us to see more.' Although he spoke impeccable English, there were moments when she was reminded of their different backgrounds. Bryn would have nudged her arm and said, 'Come on, Cass! Move your butt!' The two men couldn't have been more opposite, in other ways too. Matt's world was creative and relatively serene, whilst Bryn's had been active, constantly nudging, even inviting danger.

Soon they paused beside a red marble fountain that had been carefully restored. Matt told her that it had once been topped by the figure of Hercules.

'Why Hercules?'

'King Matthias was either shrewd or

wily, I'm not sure which. Possibly both. He pleased his nobles by depicting himself as a descendant of Attila the Hun, but he also likened himself to Hercules.' Realising with increasing pleasure that, from her rapt expression, Cass was imagining the Hungarian court of centuries ago, he went on. 'Matthias seems to have been two men: one who was determined to instil Italian culture and art in Hungary, and one who, by contrast, kept the old customs, such as eating traditional food and listening to Romany music. He founded a university, planned massive reconstruction and bridge-building projects, and yet taxed his people almost to starvation to support his massive army.'

'I think most of us are like your Hungarian king,' said Cass reflectively.

'What do you mean?' Raising one eyebrow, he looked at her in surprise.

'Don't you think we're all, in fact, two different people? The differences are easy to see when it comes to Matthias, because he had money and power. The rest of us ordinary mortals tend to be one person when we're at work. Then, when we're at home, we become someone completely different.' Her sidelong glance was mischievous. 'You, for instance, might not be the person I think you are. And I might have deep, dark secrets — for all you know, I really am Dracula's wife!'

Matt didn't laugh as she'd expected. Instead he rose and started to walk down the steps. He didn't wait to see if she followed.

'Perhaps you are feeling thirsty. Shall we find something to eat and drink?'

As he steered her towards the entrance, where earlier they had noticed several refreshment stalls, Cass couldn't help but realise he'd deliberately changed the subject. She had said something he didn't like, but she'd no idea what it was. Soon, however, he threw off any darker thoughts and bought two long bread rolls stuffed with sausage and fried onions. When he squirted his with mustard and red pepper sauce, Cass pretended to be disgusted, and then promptly did the same.

'Don't drop sauce on that beautiful

dress,' he warned, handing over an extra paper napkin. 'It will be an everlasting reminder of Visegrád, but not one you particularly want!'

They left the citadel in mid-afternoon, and at a leisurely pace drove through the sundrenched landscape, stopping occasionally to appreciate the changing view. The low convertible was ideal for such a wonderful day, thought Cass, as the breeze tugged at her scarf and threatened to play havoc with her hair. She wanted the hours to pass slowly, knowing that soon she would be returning to Budapest with Magda, and then home to England. Would she ever see Matt again? It was a question that only he could answer. She knew that if he wanted it, she would be supremely happy.

As pink and orange strands of dusk streaked the sky, they stopped at an old tavern a short distance from Szentendre. The air was cooler now, so they sat inside, watching musicians wander between the red-clothed tables, playing their wild gypsy airs. When Cass asked if they travelled from place to place around the country with their caravans and families, Matt shook his head.

'These men making music tonight would be mortally offended if you mistook them for members of the nomadic tribes. Their ancestry is very different. In the same way as the Scottish clans, each is proud of its unique heritage, and each cherishes its own culture and traditions.' As the gypsies paused beside their table, Matt tossed a coin to the woman who walked beside them with a basket of flowers. Taking a long-stemmed creamy yellow rose, he handed it to Cass. Pink-cheeked, she thanked him with a smile.

It had been a perfect day. When they returned to the car, which they had left in a place where now the moon was filtering silver threads through a lacework of trees, Matt hesitated and, almost reluctantly it seemed, drew Cass towards him. Willingly she raised her face, recognising that he was giving her a chance to pull away. His lips were gentle as they touched hers, but the moment was brief. Unbelievably, instead of following that first caress with another, deeper kiss, he slid his hands from her elbows to her shoulders and then moved her away from him. The shadows hid her bewildered eyes.

'It is time to go.' Opening the car door, he helped her into the passenger seat and silently drove back to town.

When they reached Magda's home, Matt accompanied Cass to the gate. 'Thank you for a wonderful day,' she said, and raised her face, not realising that it held an invitation he knew he should resist.

Stooping, he brushed his lips across hers. 'You helped me see the palace with fresh eyes, so it is I who should thank you.' He waited until the door opened and, with a wave, she went inside.

She could not know that as he left and drove back to the studio, his heart and his thoughts were churning as he fought the desire to turn back and say goodnight in a manner that was so very different.

★ ★ ★

The next morning, Cass came downstairs to breakfast feeling as though she was floating on air. The future beckoned, and it was bright. At least, she cautioned herself, she could face it with hope — something she hadn't known for a long time. She had no doubt that Matt liked and was attracted to her. A sensitive man, perhaps he was concerned not to rush her, knowing she was taking those first hesitant steps away from the life she had shared with Bryn.

Magda was unusually quiet as she poured coffee in the large low-ceilinged kitchen with its old-fashioned cooking range, solid table and comfortable wooden chairs. Spreading a fresh roll with apricot conserve, she bit into it, but without her normal enthusiasm. 'Did you have a good day in Visegrád?' she asked, although one glance at Cass's face had already supplied the answer.

'It was fascinating! Even though the palace is mainly ruins, you get an incredible sense of how it might have been in the past. And on the way back we stopped for dinner at one of your old inns, serenaded by gypsy violinists of course!' She didn't mention the pink rose, which she had placed carefully in a small vase beside her bed.

Magda didn't ply her with questions as she had expected. Instead, the Hungarian woman seemed engrossed in stirring her coffee. Cass frowned, concern growing as she noted her friend's downcast eyes and unsmiling mouth. 'I didn't hear you come home,' she said cautiously. 'I hope that means that you had a good time. You and Zoltan must have a lot of catching up to do.'

Magda's expression eased slightly. 'More than I could have imagined! I always liked him, and I suppose you would call him my childhood sweetheart. We lost touch, but now he has become a man who I would like to know even better.'

'Do you think he feels the same about you?'

'I hope so. I think so.'

'Then why are you so straight-faced this morning?' Cass asked bluntly. 'After all, the Fates seem to have dropped the man of your dreams right on your doorstep. What's the problem?' One idea sprang to mind. 'Is he married?'

'No.'

'Is he out of work? Would you have to support him?'

Magda shook her head. 'He has a good job at a bank in Budapest.' She paused. 'A nice safe job.' She took a deep breath and then, making up her mind, faced Cass squarely across the table. 'A nice safe, solid career,' she repeated. 'It has none of the adventure that your fiancé enjoyed.'

The glass of orange juice jerked in Cass's hand. 'What on earth?' She stared at Magda. 'What do you mean? What has Bryn's job got to do with Zoltan?'

'Nothing directly. But I have a suspicion, my friend, that you could never again bear to lose your lover so cruelly.'

'You're right,' said Cass, bewildered. What was Magda leading up to? 'I couldn't face such utter devastation a second time.'

'Then I must tell you what I heard from Zoltan last night.' As Magda searched for words, every hint of her ready laughter was absent. A bee flew through the open window and, frowning, she waited as it made its leisurely way back into the garden.

'I fear that you are becoming close to Matt,' she said reluctantly. 'But it would be best for you not to see him again. You can only be hurt.'

'What do you mean? You practically threw me at him when we first met!' Cass's voice rose. She couldn't believe her ears. 'You're forever encouraging me to find someone new, and to move on from the past!'

'Yes. But this man is wrong for you.' Magda pushed aside her plate, her food unfinished. Thrusting her hands through her dark hair, she leant her elbows on the table and sighed as though uncertain how to begin. At last she asked, 'You have heard of Lake Balaton?'

Cass nodded. She'd seen it in brochures — an enormous freshwater lake, popular with holidaymakers. What had Lake Balaton got to do with anything?

'Zoltan has a yacht which he often sails there. The other evening, I didn't realise that he also attended the concert in the square. He recognized Matthias and they talked briefly. There can be no mistake. Matt paints beautifully, as we know. But he is not an artist by profession.'

A sense of foreboding kept Cass silent. She waited. Crisp lemon-print curtains swayed slightly as a breeze relieved the heat of early morning. Magda had more to say, but her reluctance was almost tangible.

'Matt is a marine geologist who surveys ocean beds across the world,' she said at last. 'Zoltan met him two years ago at a scuba-diving conference at Lake Balaton. Matt was one of the speakers. His work on board is concerned with computers, but he spends much of his time in unknown waters.'

Diving! Ocean beds! No! Every trace of colour fled, leaving Cass parchment-white. Bryn had died rescuing a teenager from a kayak. But Bryn's had been a freak accident, a thousand-to-one chance that trapped him underwater. If Matt worked as a marine geologist, it meant the open seas, miles from land; a world in which, for Cass, the word 'safety' was an alien concept. After Bryn drowned so cruelly and so needlessly, she would forever associate water with menace and heartbreak.

It wasn't fair! Never again! How could she let herself care for a man whose work took him into perilous waters, uncharted territories? Another man who seemingly revelled in skimming the surface of danger? She didn't realise she had spoken.

'You say, 'No, never again!" Magda's eyelashes were wet as she jumped up and came around the table to hug Cass. 'I am so very sorry! But I knew I must tell you before you lost your heart.'

It was too late for that! Cass had known yesterday that she'd fallen head over heels in love with Matt. They'd only met a few days ago, but she knew that he was everything she wanted. And, despite his hesitancy, she was sure he felt the same. In the early hours she had lain awake, imagining a future that could hold the two of them together. Scorning herself for such teenage dreams, still she'd been unable to resist them. As an artist, Matt would be free to work anywhere. If he preferred to stay in Hungary, then perhaps she could find a job teaching English at a language college here. Magda had enjoyed her work in England; Cass would do the same, but in Matt's homeland.

Now there was a bitter taste inside her mouth, and a new, corrosive feeling of hurt. He'd allowed her to believe his life was what she had seen; that he was content to earn a living with his canvases and paints. It was utterly different from the truth. What a fool she'd been! Why had he pretended to be an artist? Then, with painful honesty, she had to admit that he'd never pretended. He *was* an artist. She'd assumed that it was his only occupation. How could anyone be so wrong?

She pushed back her soft fringe with

fingers that were frozen, despite the warmth of the room. Magda was making a poor pretence of resuming her breakfast. She had clearly hated breaking this news, but Cass knew that she'd felt it essential.

There was only one comfort. Matt had no idea that Cassandra Sutherland, a little history teacher from England, had fallen in love with him. When she left Szentendre, he would think she'd merely been flirting. He knew as little about her as she had known about him. No, that wasn't true. She'd told him about Bryn and the dangers of his job. Surely that was the time when Matt should have revealed that his own work was even more hazardous?

The kitchen was silent whilst Magda, her face unusually sombre, reheated the coffee pot. 'Zoltan must return to Budapest later today,' she said, seemingly concerned only with refilling their cups. 'He has offered to take us, if we can be ready by mid-afternoon.'

'I'll fall in with whatever you suggest.' Cass curled her fingers around the warmth of her cup, wishing it could relieve the chill in her heart as well. 'But this morning I shall need to see Matt and tell him we're leaving.' Her lips felt stiff; her eyes were wide and saw nothing. Even now, hoping for a miracle, she asked, 'Was Zoltan certain?'

Magda nodded unhappily. 'When he spoke to Matt and Anna at the concert, they said Matt was recovering from an illness. They were reticent about his plans but eventually said he hopes to return to sea next month.'

$$\star \quad \star \quad \star$$

It was the end of her new, shining world, realised Cass later as she passed along the street towards Anna's studio. Berating herself, she wondered how she could have relaxed her defences so completely with a man she scarcely knew. No wonder he'd become silent when she joked that each of them was two people, and that her other self might be Dracula's wife! Bitterly she realised that he had far more to hide than she did. How could he have made love to her in words, in attitude, even a light kiss? She'd told him about Bryn, and had put the gentleness of that kiss, the holding back, down to sensitivity; a fear of rushing her. Why had he sought her company and made her feel that he cared? Surely he realised she couldn't risk such loss ever again?

Anna was in the courtyard, alone. When she saw Cass she came towards her, hands outstretched, although her greeting was muted.

'Good morning, Cassandra!' Today, like Magda, there was no smile. This was unusual, because Anna was invariably cheerful. An appealing dimple would appear in her cheek when something amused her, and lively, expressive eyes revealed a woman who was relaxed and happy in her family life. Her normal open friendliness was restrained as she said, 'I am glad you enjoyed your day at Visegrád.'

'Thank you. It was an enjoyable history lesson,' said Cass. And that was all it had been, she told herself. 'I came to thank

Matt again for being such an excellent guide.'

'Matt is not here.' Anna paused. Like Magda earlier, she appeared hesitant, and to be searching for the right words. What was wrong with everyone today? 'A message arrived while he was at Visegrád with you. An urgent business matter obliged him to leave here late last night. He asked me to give you his heartfelt apologies and to say that he will contact you as soon as possible, although by then you may have returned to Budapest.' Avoiding Cass's gaze, she fussed unnecessarily with postcards on an ornamental display stand. 'Or maybe you will be in England. He did not know how long he would be away.'

'That's a coincidence!' said Cass lightly, drawing on all her reserves of pride. 'As well as thanking him for yesterday, I came to say goodbye. I'm leaving Szentendre today because Magda's friend has offered us a lift to Budapest. We'll stay there a day or two, and then head back to England.' She managed a laugh, although to her own ears it sounded brittle. 'I hope Matt's business problems are resolved quickly.' Slyly she added, 'He'll be longing to get back here to his painting,' and then immediately felt ashamed as colour flooded Anna's face. The Hungarian obviously hated being deceitful, and it was obvious that Matt had warned her to say nothing of his plans.

Although Anna offered coffee, she couldn't hide her relief when Cass declined. 'Thanks, but no thanks. I must go and pack.' Shaking Anna's hand, Cass avoided the hug which the other woman obviously intended. 'Give my love to Lili, and a big kiss. It was wonderful to meet you both.'

By mid-afternoon, Cass was seated in Zoltan's car, heading away from Szentendre and heartache.

4

England seemed particularly grey and wet this evening, thought Cass as she shook out her tartan umbrella before unlocking the door of her flat. Shrugging off her raincoat, she hung it above the radiator, which was just starting to warm the tiny entrance hall. Running cold fingers through her damp hair, she stared at the sombre woman looking back from the mirror, face wiped clear of any animation. The downward curve of her lips said it all. Ever since leaving Hungary three months ago, there was no sunshine in her heart, whatever the weather.

There had been no word from Matt. By mutual, unspoken consent, neither she nor Magda mentioned him. It was particularly hard to forget their holiday and the man who had stolen her heart, because Zoltan often flew from Budapest to spend a few days with Magda, so inevitably Cass saw him. She was happy for her friend. The couple were well-matched; and, she thought, not without a hint of cynicism, they had an added advantage. Knowing each other since childhood, there were no dark secrets to hide.

Her appetite had deserted her these days, so after a sparse supper of pasta and salad, Cass settled down to a pile of essay-marking. She had scarcely started when her doorbell rang. With a sigh, she laid down the exercise book she'd been working on and went to see which of her neighbours had forgotten their key, needed computer help or, more probably, enough coffee to last till morning.

It was Matt. He stood there, tall and lean, with rain sparkling on his dark hair and shoulders. His smile was the same, but the gaunt look had gone from his face, and he was lightly tanned. Perhaps unsure of his welcome, the smile faded when she said nothing.

'May I come in?'

Cass stood back, wordless, as he stepped forward, shrinking her small hallway.

'Have you eaten?' he asked as though they had been together only yesterday.

She nodded, and then cleared her throat. 'Yes.' Was this how it felt to lose all power of thought? Pulling her wits together, she automatically said, 'I mean yes, I've had supper, but maybe I can get you something? It won't take long.'

He shook his head. 'No, thank you. I had a big lunch, and then a snack just an hour ago.' His lopsided smile appeared again. 'Not hot dogs. And no tomato relish.'

'I'm glad to hear it.' Why did he want to remind her of that sun-filled day when they'd wandered around the ruins of Visegrád?

He hung his damp coat on a spare peg and followed as, mouth dry, limbs stiff, Cass walked into her sitting room. As she indicated her big armchair and he sat down, looking around with interest, she shook her head as though waking from a deep sleep. What were they doing here, making polite conversation? It seemed that he thought the same, because his blue-grey eyes were intent, his manner unusually hesitant.

Matt had known this meeting would be difficult, but the reality was worse than he'd imagined. How could he find a way to penetrate the protective cloak of reserve that Cass was wearing? That fine-boned innate dignity reminded him of the first time they'd met: whilst Magda tried to flirt, Cass had remained a background figure, so different from the laughing, easy companion of later days.

'I have come to apologise for disappearing so unexpectedly while you were in Szentendre.'

About time too! Cass didn't answer. The words sounded genuine enough, but how was she meant to respond? In any case, her heart was thumping so loudly that surely it would drown anything she said. She must have sat again in the smaller armchair beside the exercise books, or perhaps her legs simply collapsed beneath her. When she said nothing, after a few long, waiting seconds, Matt broke the silence.

'Anna will have told you that after that wonderful day at the old citadel, when I returned home I found an urgent message that made it necessary for me to leave immediately. It would have been impossible to tell you the true reason, and I could not lie. All I could do was go. When I returned to Szentendre, weeks later, Anna told me that she knew Zoltan was regularly visiting England and your friend Magda. I realised you would hear of my marine work from them.

'I'd already planned to follow you to England as soon as possible and tell you about my real career. So now, here at last, I must say how sorry I am. But it was an essential subterfuge.' His voice deepened, intensifying the slight accent which was always there. 'I did not want to deceive you, but had no choice.' A rueful glint lit his eyes and his mouth registered self-mockery. 'I can earn a reasonable living from painting pretty pictures for the tourists, but have a long way to go before I rival Van Gogh's immortal sunflowers!'

Cass found her voice at last, although her throat felt as though it had been sandpapered. 'Why didn't you? Tell me, I mean.' Though desperate to learn his answer, she didn't yet feel ready to hear it. His arrival this evening had turned her world upside down; a world which she had tried unsuccessfully to manicure into some semblance of calm; a world where no strong emotions were allowed. She dreaded any return to those turbulent days she had suffered before meeting him, as well as during these past three months, when to let herself feel anything was to know hurt and loss.

Desperately summoning a semblance of hospitality, and with it the security of nondescript daily life, she asked, 'Before you tell me what you've been doing, can I get you something to drink?'

'Coffee would be welcome.'

Matt followed her into the galley-shaped kitchen while she filled the kettle, and then he wandered back into the other room, inspecting her books and ornaments. Deep amber velvet curtains were drawn, shutting out the November gloom. A log-effect gas fire cast its glow across a couch which promised comfort, with a creamy throw and jewel-bright cushions. Ranged beside the fire, where Cass had been sitting, Matt saw a footstool and round wooden coffee table cluttered with papers and exercise books. More exam-marking? he wondered with a slight smile.

There was no sign of the landscape she'd bought from him that first day. Wryly, he guessed it was probably still wrapped, buried deep in some cupboard. Or maybe she had set a match to it! Perhaps he shouldn't have come until his business was settled. But it had become impossible to keep away, now that investigations were underway and to some extent the need for secrecy had lifted.

When they were both seated, Cass looked at him enquiringly. Again, speech seemed to have deserted her. And there was the danger that, if she did speak, she would reveal too much. He'd deceived and hurt her, and the pain was still there.

'Where do I begin?' Matt stretched out his long legs and raked a hand through his hair. It needed cutting, she thought with swift tenderness as he pushed back a dark lock that had fallen over his brow. It was one of the things she'd remembered, that habit of his, as well as the way he would run one long finger along his jaw when something perplexed him. He was doing it now, a sign that he wasn't confident about her reaction. Or perhaps he wasn't sure how much to tell her.

Mentally, Cass shook herself. *Give him a chance! Listen, and then sort out the truth from any lies.* Attack was the only defence — this was no time for sentiment. Even though all she wanted was to throw herself into Matt's arms and beg him never to leave her again! She must try to sound noncommittal, whatever he had to disclose. It might be best simply to say she'd been annoyed that he hadn't been honest. Why had he led her to believe he earned a living by painting pictures, when all the time he was a highly trained professional with a technological career?

Or was it scientific? Or a bit of each? She hadn't a clue — and right now she didn't care.

Carefully, she made her expression blank and avoided his eyes by leaning forward to straighten one of the papers on the coffee table. 'Zoltan recognised you as a marine geologist,' she said. 'Why did you pretend to be an artist?' Secretly she congratulated herself on taking the initiative.

Matt set down his coffee mug and leaned back in his chair, relaxing slightly. He felt slow relief creeping through his limbs at the prospect of being open with her at last. Deception wasn't one of his normal characteristics, and it hadn't come easily.

'I *am* an artist! And I enjoy it!' He grinned like a boy, his eyes clear, his expression straightforward. 'But my real job, one I studied for years to achieve, is in hydrographic engineering or its associate, marine geology. Even from early childhood the subject fascinated me, and the happiest day of my life was when I first began to explore the mysteries hidden deep on the floor of the world's oceans.'

He gestured towards the pile of exercise books. 'As a teacher, you will understand how vital such research can be. The earth's plates are constantly shifting, and we need to be forewarned about natural disasters such as earthquakes. Also, of course, in this modern world, governments take increasing interest in what lies beneath the surface of the water. International boundaries are studied and disputed as never before. There's immense wealth to be found in oil and mineral deposits.'

'Why were you so secretive?' Slowly, almost reluctantly, Cass, too, was relaxing under the obvious truth of his explanation, but needed more before her heart would allow complete trust.

He sighed and ran one hand around the back of his neck. This was the first time Cass had seen him in formal clothes. He had already loosened his tie slightly, as though he wasn't used to its constriction, and his white shirt and elegant suit made him almost a stranger. Sharply she reminded herself that he *was* a stranger. The man she'd met in Szentendre was an artist.

'It's a long story,' said Matt thoughtfully, 'and the final chapter is still incomplete. Basically, I am employed by a marine survey company that is based in London. We work under contract for governments across the globe. Each ship has captain and crew, and is loaded with intricate equipment used by hydrographic surveyors who work in conjunction with marine geologists.'

Cass looked perplexed. He watched her changing expressions with a sympathetic smile as he tried to explain, his eyes lighting with enthusiasm as he sought the right words. 'In simple terms, hydrographic surveyors plot the contours of the ocean bed, and marine geologists try to discover its composition. Where territorial boundaries of certain countries meet, there can be disputes, some of them serious.'

'I can understand that, especially where there are potentially valuable deposits.' As that earlier resentment began to fade, Cass realised with growing interest that more than simple deception was involved in Matt's earlier need to hide his true career.

He nodded and continued, 'We had been working from our ship, the *Venus.* We were a few miles off the African shore, investigating ancient beach terraces. You often find minerals in these, thanks to erosion from volcanic areas inland. Their sediment is carried down to sea by the rivers. Most of our analysis is done on board ship, thanks to state-of-the-art computer systems, but occasionally we decide that we want to take a closer look, and dive.' He took a long breath, and his jaw tightened as she listened. Deep-seated anger was easy to see in his expression, and in the words that came harshly across the room.

'My partner, Paul, and I discovered possible diamond deposits almost three hundred metres down. Secrecy was essential until we had a chance to investigate more thoroughly. The only person we told was Ben Holmes, our hydrographic surveyor. A computer malfunction on board meant that, temporarily, our location hadn't been recorded, so there was no tracking record. Unfortunately, I, plus a couple of our team, went down with a bug we'd possibly picked up from a stopover in Mombasa. It was a nasty bacterial infection that unfortunately knocked me completely out of action. We had a medic on board, but with only limited resources, so I had to leave the ship and get more intensive treatment than he could provide.' His face darkened still more. 'This meant that Paul was obliged to work underwater with a stranger, a fellow recommended by Holmes.'

Suddenly Matt jumped up, as though he couldn't tolerate sitting still. He moved to the window and pushed the curtain aside, to look into the street. Outside, all was dark, apart from the glow of a streetlamp which sparkled neighbouring rooftops in the light rain.

'Paul dived. He blacked out when he was ten metres down. His equipment had been sabotaged. The new man,

Hans, continued the dive alone, although he must have known that Paul was in trouble. The fact that he didn't sound the alarm, or help, was damning!' Releasing the curtain, he swung back into the room, hands thrust into trouser pockets, his eyebrows a straight black line.

'What happened?' This was the last thing that Cass had expected. 'Is Paul all right?'

'Thank God, he's recovering at last.' The frown lifted slightly as Matt settled back into his chair. A swift thought came to Cass, even as she listened. He looked ... right, as though that side of the fireplace was naturally his. All it needed was a scatter of newspapers and soft shoes, even slippers. She shook away the image.

Matt was continuing, 'When Paul's gear was checked, they found that the filter had been removed from his compressor so that it let in carbon monoxide. This meant that soon after starting his dive, he found he couldn't breathe. Before he could raise the alarm, he blacked out. Thank heaven one of the crew realised there was a problem and pulled him up, but Paul was seriously ill. For weeks he had to be kept in a medically induced coma.'

'Do you know who damaged his equipment?' Cass stopped short. 'I'm being stupid! It was Hans, of course. It could have been murder!'

He inclined his head. 'There is fierce competition, of course, for precious finds. And diamonds talk money, wherever you are! The ship's captain contacted me when I was in Szentendre, recovering from my own illness, and in the meantime helping Anna. The call came through while you were at the studio.'

Cass recalled the moment when Matt had returned to the courtyard, obviously angered by news he'd received, but keen to set it aside in her presence.

Matt went on, 'He'd made quiet enquiries of his own and discovered that Hans, the man brought in by Holmes, had been part of a team involved in a previous marine diving 'accident'.' Grim-faced, he added, 'When Hans continued the dive alone, it was to obtain a sample that he could pass to an international company, unscrupulous and no stranger to dirty dealings.'

'Why did you have to lie low?'

'Before I collapsed with that damned bug, I managed to send a private message to our London manager. So only he knew about a possible deposit of diamonds, apart from Paul and me — and, of course, Ben Holmes. After what happened to Paul, we knew that I, too, could be at risk, simply because I was the most likely to recognise its location in the depths of the Indian Ocean. Computers are great when they're functioning; and in this instance, of course, failure ensured that no one beyond the *Venus* could access the precise position. It was a stroke of luck for us. Others might spend a fortune hunting for it, eventually find the spot, and the 'diamonds' turn out to be as worthless as a rusty bucket. You've heard of industrial espionage, but even men as ruthless as this have to watch their purse-strings!'

Cass found that she'd been holding her

breath. 'What will happen now?'

'Ben Holmes finally admitted that he'd been approached by outsiders. He's close to retirement, and the money was tempting. But at heart he's a decent man, and couldn't stand the guilt of what he'd done to Paul. Naively, he hadn't realised that for high stakes, murder means nothing to men who scent riches.'

'What about Hans?'

Matt's lips twisted in disgust as he jumped up from his chair again and strode from one side of the room to the other. 'Hans has disappeared.' He flung his arms wide in total exasperation. 'He might resurface in a year or so. The authorities will keep close watch.'

'And what about your find on the seabed?'

'We're not yet certain, but it seems likely that we located quite a large diamond field. If the results are positive, a decision will be made about legal ownership.'

'So you've possibly found diamonds, Paul is recovering, one baddie has repented, and the other has done a bunk.'

Laughter smoothed the lines beside his mouth. 'As your English saying goes — in a nutshell, yes.'

'Then 'All's well that ends well',' as our equally English Shakespeare would say.' Cass stood and picked up the empty coffee mugs, ready to take them into the kitchen. The small act relieved some of the tension that was building inside her as she realised that, explanations over, it was inevitable that they would move on to more personal issues.

'Not quite.' Matt's eyes were serious. 'I didn't intentionally deceive you, although that is how it must seem. You knew me as an artist, and I think we had found something rare and special.'

'Not special enough to tell me the truth.'

He shook his head and came closer, taking the mugs from her. One stride took him to the kitchen, and when he returned he took her hands in his. 'When you said that we were each two different people, I was sorely tempted. But I dared not speak. Vast amounts of money were at stake, and it's a sad reality that there are many evil men and corporations in the world. The fewer people who knew, the safer those people would remain.' His expression pleaded with her to understand as he continued. 'I was concerned for Anna, but she and her husband were insistent that I must stay with them, and that no one would take notice of an old school-friend who worked as an artist.' Tightening his grasp a little, he said, 'I trusted you but could not put you at risk.'

'Well, I'm grateful that you've taken the trouble to come and tell me now,' said Cass, gently disengaging her hands and returning to what felt like familiar, and safe, territory beside the fire. 'When do you return to sea?'

Matt's eyelids flickered as he registered her dismissively brisk tone and deliberate glance at the pile of school books beside her chair.

'Soon.' He came to stand before her, understanding in his eyes, one hand outstretched. 'Before then, I want to persuade you to spend time with the man who is a marine geologist. You already know the artist.' There was tenderness in his eyes and in his deep voice as he looked down at the fair head, so deliberately turned away. 'When I first saw you, it was as though I had been waiting for you all my life. I feel that I know you so well, but now I would like to show you the real man behind the smokescreen.'

With an immense effort, Cass rose to her feet, so that he was obliged to move away, his hand dropping to his side. Her wayward heart urged one response, but her head warned her otherwise. Forcing all expression from her white face, she looked deliberately into Matt's eyes, praying that he would accept her decision.

'I'm sorry, but I'm particularly busy this term at school,' she said coolly. 'When I met you I was on holiday.' Glad that he couldn't know how much willpower it took to steady her voice, ruefully she admitted, 'I was attracted to the man I met in Szentendre, the artist who could talk and laugh with me.'

'A man you could perhaps love? One

who had fallen in love with you?'

Her colour rose, but she met his intent gaze bravely. 'A man I could quite easily love.'

'But what of the other man? All that is different is the way he earns a living.'

'You say 'all that is different'! Even though I told you about Bryn.' She stepped back.

Despite every fibre in his body silently calling to her, he knew that her mind was closing against him.

'And let's face it,' she said, 'there's little point in me getting to know a marine geologist, since he'll be working on board ship most of the time!'

'And could drown?' He was purposefully cruel.

Her face blanched, but she faced him squarely. 'And could drown.'

Within minutes, she stood alone at the window. He had gone.

Again and again, Cass asked herself if she had expected Matt to try and persuade her. Finally she acknowledged that, from the beginning, one of the things she had loved was his sensitivity. She had told him enough of her feelings. With the right man — and he was the right man — she could love freely. But love wasn't enough. She couldn't bear to live on a knife-edge, always waiting for news that there'd been an accident, and that he was dead — fathoms down, in some unknown sea. All the old pain came back; the anguish that had haunted her for so long. Could she ever forget Bryn's beloved face as they'd fought, helpless to stop relentless coils from dragging him down?

At last the tears came. The agony of loss was something she could never bear to suffer again. Never.

5

Christmas came and went. What Cass really wanted was to hide in her wardrobe until it was over, but there was no escape. Luckily, school festivities meant that she was busy with carol services, parties and end-of-term plays. The block of flats where she lived was quiet, almost deserted. Magda had flown to Budapest to spend the holiday with her parents and Zoltan. It seemed probable that when she returned, she would be wearing an engagement ring, and that her teaching days in England were numbered. Cass was happy for her, but knew that when the time came, she'd sadly miss someone who had become a good friend.

It was impossible to refuse an invitation to spend Christmas with her father and stepmother. Perhaps, however, because she'd dreaded it, the holiday was surprisingly enjoyable. Liz was the sort of woman who fitted comfortably into her role as wife to an older man. At the same time, she was genuinely welcoming to Cass, and made it clear that she understood, and didn't resent, the bond between daughter and father.

At fifty, Peter Sutherland had the appearance of a younger man. Tall and well-built, his movements were purposeful and hinted at earlier years when he had been a keen sportsman. He still played tennis regularly, and it was at a local club that he'd first encountered Liz.

Liz, at thirty-five, was fifteen years her husband's junior, but the age difference was scarcely noticeable. She worked as a buyer for the fashion section of a department store, and Cass had no doubt that she was good at her job. 'Businesslike, but without crackle' was how she'd described Liz to a friend. Almost as tall as her husband, Liz's slender figure was invariably dressed in stylish and yet unobtrusive clothes in shades of brown and burnt orange that complemented her sleek chestnut hair and hazel eyes. She had an infectious laugh and a dry sense of humour that ensured a loyal circle of friends, who soon extended a welcome to Cass.

The festive period was pleasantly sociable. Cass was always glad to see David, her unmarried uncle, and liked Liz's brother Reg, who came to dinner with Molly, his wife. There were invitations from neighbours, and friends came for drinks or to eat at the house Peter Sutherland had bought when he remarried. Another break with the past, but Cass accepted that it was right for him and Liz. She knew how deeply he'd mourned her mother and cared for her through the final heartbreaking months of her cruel illness. But, loving him as she did, she was glad that he'd finally moved on to a new life, and renewed happiness.

Cass stayed several days longer than planned, glad to spend time with her father, and enjoying Liz's company. Her stepmother was keen to visit the winter sales and, Cass knew, wouldn't be able to resist the fashion aisles.

'All right! I know you're having a quiet laugh!' Eyes dancing, Liz pushed through the barrier at the Underground station. 'Call it a busman's holiday!'

After a few hours, thoroughly pleased with their bargains, they decided on a late lunch at a bistro where Cass often ate with friends. By chance, two were there today, equally footsore, laden with shopping, so the four shared a table. Sitting, they sent up a mutual groan of relief.

'Don't take your shoes off, whatever you do!' warned Liz. 'You'll never get them on again!'

Val and Tricia both taught at the same school as Cass and had previously met and obviously liked Liz, so conversation was easy. It was a good day, and Cass's spirits felt higher than they had for months.

On her final evening, she was packing her suitcase when Peter Sutherland tapped on the bedroom door. When she called out to him, he entered, carrying a small velvet-covered jewel case. Inscribed on the lid were the initials 'HS'.

'I want you to have this, Cassandra,'

he said. 'It belonged to your mother.' He smiled slightly as, smoothing the lid with gentle fingers, he confessed, 'I should've given it to you several years ago, but to tell the truth, I couldn't bring myself to part with it.'

As he placed the box in her hands, Cass shook her head, visibly touched, and tried to return it. She had a few keepsakes that were precious, even though the memory of her mother and the illness that eventually defeated her had become less painful as time went by.

'No, Dad, you keep it. This belongs to the part of your life that you shared with Mum.'

He pushed it gently back to her. 'I don't need tangible reminders of your mother. She's in my heart and always will be. I'm not giving you this because Liz is my wife now — she knows I love her, but understands that I can never discard my memories. She wouldn't want me to. After all, my marriage to Helen, and then the joy we shared when you were born, are what made me the person I am today.'

Moving closer, he gave Cass a hug. His thick blue jumper was soft and warm, and she took a deep breath of the scent that she'd always associated with her father. It was a mixture of the tangy aftershave he favoured, the logs that he'd loaded ready for their sitting-room fire that evening, and an even more evocative smell of mild peppermint — his particular weakness, despite the teasing he endured.

Leaning his cheek on her hair, he said quietly, 'I loved your mother so much that it took years before I could open my heart to another woman. When I met Liz, it was almost impossible to believe that happiness would come my way again.' Releasing Cass, he took hold of her shoulders and looked into the grey eyes so like his own. His were searching and concerned. 'I don't want you to lose too many precious years mourning Bryn. At least I had you to love and care for, which helped ease the pain of losing Helen.'

He watched the expressions that crossed her face and knew she was close to tears. After a moment he said carefully,

'I've a feeling that your trip to Hungary unsettled you for some reason. I don't want to pry, my love. But I worry about you.'

Cass blinked away the moisture before it spilled. Suddenly it was infinitely sweet to feel that she was a child again, safe in her father's care. 'There's nothing that need bother you, Dad.' Burying her face in his shoulder, her voice was muffled. 'I'll admit that I met someone I thought I could be happy with, but his life and mine could never match. That's all.'

'I see.' She had a feeling that her father saw more than the bald statement, but he didn't ask questions, for which she was thankful.

When she opened the jewellery case later, she found several rings and necklaces which she remembered seeing her mother wear on special occasions. It was a relief that although the old sadness lingered and would never completely fade, she could touch them with loving fingers and remember the special moments.

* * *

The January term started as usual, but then came such heavy falls of snow that her school was forced to close for several days. Cass found it irksome to be trapped inside her small flat, although she would normally enjoy the unexpected break from work. She made a point of going out, despite the treacherous icy pavements, to meet friends for coffee or a snack.

On the third day she even went sledging with an old schoolmate, Marion, who had ten-year-old twins and a house in leafy suburbs within easy reach of central London. A big-hearted woman, she ran an animal ambulance service and was quick to remind friends that they mustn't part with their belongings, unless it was to the charity's shop. Despite her loyal group of volunteers, at weekends or school holidays she sometimes hauled Cass in as an extra, either in the shop, sorting and serving, or even helping collect injured animals. Her husband likened their house to a zoo, but it was a welcome haven that day after a couple of hours in the snow. Tingling with cold, everyone was glad of the hot soup and rolls she magically produced. When Cass complimented her, she confessed that it wasn't down to wizardry, but to the flasks she'd filled earlier.

A ring at the doorbell announced Richard, Marion's brother. Cass had known him for years and liked him, so didn't hesitate when a few days later he telephoned to ask if she would like to go to the theatre. The play had received excellent reviews, Richard was good company, and she enjoyed herself. When he asked her out to dinner the following week, she was happy to go. It was easy to relax with him, perhaps because her heart wasn't involved. There was safety, too, because he'd recently parted with a long-term girlfriend, and she guessed he was in no hurry for anything more than friend-ship. Stockily built and sandy-haired, he had such an engaging smile and attractive personality that she couldn't believe he'd remain unattached for long.

As expected, Magda returned from her Christmas holiday in Budapest wearing a diamond engagement ring. Less expected was the news that she and Zoltan planned to marry in early summer.

'We can't afford to spend a fortune on travel,' she explained. 'It will cost too much to keep flying to see each other. The money would be better spent on buying somewhere to live, although we might have to rent at first.'

'I shall miss you,' Cass told her. It was true. For a fleeting, despondent moment, Cass wondered if this was how it would always be — that she would grow close to people, only to lose them.

'And I shall miss you, my friend, but there will always be a bed for you wherever we live.' Magda's dark eyes were laughing. 'So long as you make it yourself, and then do my housework!' She dodged the cushion that sailed across the room towards her.

6

Cass couldn't believe that she was here, in Szentendre, once more. She'd thought never to see the small riverside town again. Being the original home of Magda's parents and Zoltan's family also, it was the natural venue for a traditional Hungarian wedding, rather than the civil ceremony that was more common in many of the larger cities.

Magda had said farewell to her college colleagues in England and travelled to Szentendre a week ago in order to prepare for the big day. Her parents' house was too small to accommodate many visitors, so they had reserved rooms in a nearby hotel for several who would need to stay overnight or longer. By erecting a marquee on the grounds, the hotel would also cater for the reception after the ceremony.

On the evening of her arrival, Cass was obliged to pass Anna's studio as she went with Magda and her cousin Sophie to the terrace café where they had arranged to meet other guests. Streets and squares, and the riverside walk, were bright with the blossoms and atmosphere she remembered so well. Was it almost a year ago that she'd been here? It seemed more like a lifetime. And in that time she had scaled the heights, dreaming of a future that could hold Matt, only to plummet to the depths of despair once again.

Although it was still only spring, the days were pleasantly warm and the summer heat yet to come. A number of tourists were wandering in and out of shops and restaurants, enjoying the warm, dry air as the sun sank, turning the sky to pink-gold, and dusk slowly fell. Cass turned her head away from the court-yard. She'd taken care to steer Magda and Sophie to the far side of the street, and Magda, sensitively, had allowed herself to be steered. It was very likely that even at this hour, Anna would hope to attract passers-by with her display of paintings, pottery, local souvenirs and postcards. Fervently Cass hoped that Matt's Hungarian friend would be busy with customers, too busy to notice her.

Her heart yearned to see him standing there, selling his canvases. But her head said, *You've put Matthias Benedek behind you. Be thankful that he's not here to tempt you again with his blue-grey eyes, his lopsided smile, his kissable mouth and his heartbreaking ways.*

The wedding day was cloudless and the temperature perfect for guests in their formal wear, although Cass noticed one or two men surreptitiously undoing the top button of their shirts, hidden beneath formal ties. A number of women wore traditional embroidered blouses and braided skirts, with beribboned headdresses. Others had opted for light gauzy chiffons or fine cotton outfits with wide-brimmed headwear that threatened to take flight in the occasional breeze.

Cass wore a silk dress in her favourite shade of cornflower blue. Bringing a hat from England hadn't been a practical option, so instead she'd pinned a cluster of tiny blue and white daisies in her hair and prayed that they would stay in place.

The bride and her father arrived in the pony and trap, now gaily decorated with white flowers and wide satin ribbons, which Cass had seen waiting for customers when she was previously here. Magda looked enchanting. A white lace bridal gown complemented her gleaming hair and shapely figure, and love shone from her radiant face as Zoltan turned to greet her at the altar of the ancient church. Following her up the aisle came two young bridesmaids in a froth of creamy tulle and flowered headdresses, who managed to behave impeccably, although Cass suspected their parents were on tenterhooks until release came at the end of the service.

Anna was sitting halfway down the nave with Lili and a man who was presumably her husband, Istvan. Magda had warned Cass that they'd be present, having come face-to-face with Anna at the market a few days ago. A discreet enquiry had revealed that Matt was working abroad, so with her usual impulsive generosity Magda had invited Anna, Istvan and Lili to the wedding. Cass knew it was unlikely that she could avoid them altogether, but hoped there wouldn't be time to exchange more than a few greetings. She slipped into a pew at the back of the church, and at the reception was relieved to find herself seated some distance away from the family who were so closely linked with Matt.

Afterwards, whilst the terrace of the hotel was being prepared for dancing, Cass wandered a little way from the rest of the guests. People were friendly, but it was a family occasion and she didn't want anyone to feel obliged to speak English, although many were so fluent that she felt ashamed of knowing so few Hungarian words. Last year Magda had rehearsed her pronunciation of please, thank you, yes and no before deciding that Cass was hopeless, and telling her to manage as best she could.

The rise and fall of conversation was pleasant, even if she didn't understand more than a word or two, but she was content to be alone. Magda and Zoltan would leave early next morning to spend a quiet honeymoon beside Lake Balaton. Having travelled so much recently in order to spend time together either in Budapest or in London, they would go further afield for a longer holiday later in the year.

Being in Szentendre was even more difficult than Cass had feared. In London it was easy enough to turn her thoughts from disturbing images. Here, they were uncomfortably real. She felt that she only had to look over her shoulder and Matt would be leaning over the stone balustrade, picking a spray of bougainvillea to tuck into her hair. Or perhaps she'd watch him smothering another hot-dog roll with bright red ketchup as he had on that wonderful day in Visegrád.

Lost in memory, it was a shock to hear a voice and, turning, find Anna standing behind her. The Hungarian woman's smile was friendly, but less certain than it had been last summer. Today she wore traditional costume, with its full braided skirt and exquisitely embroidered puff-sleeved blouse. Not conventionally attractive, she possessed an indefinable charm. Cass knew she must be roughly the same age as Matt, about thirty, or slightly less. She often looked younger, although tiny lines radiating from the corners of her eyes made her appear older when her face was serious, as it was now.

'I am happy to see you, Cassandra.' Anna offered Cass her hand and enquired about her journey from England. 'Will you stay in Szentendre for a few days after the wedding?' she asked politely. She seemed restrained, as though slightly unsure of her welcome. Cass suspected that a few months ago Anna would have greeted her with obvious delight, a kiss and a hug. Hurriedly, she pulled herself together.

'No, unfortunately I have to go home tomorrow because there's work to prepare for the start of term.' It wasn't strictly true. Cass could have delayed her return to England for a few days, but didn't want to impose on Magda's parents, and had no wish to stay in Hungary alone — and, cried her heart, without Matt. 'Where is Lili?' She looked beyond Anna, but the child and her father were nowhere to be seen. Cass had caught a glimpse of him taking photographs outside the church: a well-built man with close-cropped fair hair.

'My daughter is busy playing with the bridesmaids.' Anna's face lit to laughter as she swung to scan the terrace and landscaped gardens. 'They survived the speeches well, but were glad to escape.' She looked around again. 'My husband is somewhere with his new toy, a very up-to-date digital camera.' Mischievously she added, 'I suspect he has taken two hundred photos, to be reduced to a respectable thirty or so!' She glanced at her wristwatch. 'We shall stay a short time for the dancing, but must leave by early evening because Istvan is piloting a dawn flight tomorrow. You may remember I told you that he works for a small airline, just a few miles distant.'

'Well, it's lovely to see you again, Anna,' said Cass somewhat untruthfully. She liked Matt's friend, but didn't want to return to anything that might seem like the old easy relationship they'd shared. Maybe in another year or two the memory of their courtyard coffees and conversation wouldn't affect her so deeply. Not that she planned ever to return here.

Anna made no move to leave. She looked as though she was about to say something, but didn't quite know where to start. There was an awkward silence until Cass hurried to end it. She liked Anna so much, and hated the thought of parting without even a trace of the camaraderie they'd once shared.

'Magda told me about one of your traditions, the bride's dance,' she said, searching her brain for some innocuous comment.

'Yes, although I doubt that we shall see one today.' Anna relaxed slightly, looking rueful. 'It can be an expensive business!'

'People used to pay to dance with the bride?'

'The newlyweds sometimes collected enough money for the deposit on a house! That is a tradition which has almost disappeared in these straightened times, I fear.'

Again there was a short silence. Then Anna appeared to make up her mind. Her eyes were earnest as she lightly touched Cass's arm. 'Cassandra, I must speak to you about Matthias. He is deeply unhappy that he did not tell you the truth about his work when you were together in Szentendre.'

'It was unfortunate. But I understand that it was necessary.' Cass couldn't keep the stiffness from her voice. She simply didn't want to talk about Matt or last summer.

'He was obliged to be silent,' said Anna, even now speaking softly. 'He had no choice. But the problem has been resolved.' Hesitantly she said, 'I think he told you something of what happened.'

'Yes. You obviously know that he visited me in London.' For one passing second, Cass envied the other woman's longstanding friendship with Matt. By contrast, Cass herself knew virtually nothing about his early life, his family, or his growing-up years. On that day in Visegrád, when she asked about his family, he merely said that his father had been an architect who died shortly after Matt graduated from university. His mother remarried a year later and lived in Bermuda now, and he saw her rarely. He appeared reluctant to enlarge on his background, so she'd let the subject drop. Now, however, here with Anna, she wished she'd pressed him to talk more, but it didn't feel right to ask, and the moment passed.

'Has his partner fully recovered?' Matt would have brought Anna up to date with news of Paul's health.

'I am glad to say that Paul is well, and with Matthias again. He had a lucky escape.'

'Matt spoke of industrial espionage,' said Cass thoughtfully. In the dark reaches of so many nights, she had realised how he'd been caught up in events completely beyond his control. 'I suppose this is a real-life example. It's not confined to James Bond films.'

'No,' said Anna, laughing slightly. 'But all is well. The deposits Matt and Paul discovered have been analysed. They are diamonds, possibly from a field of moderate size, and legally the property of the government which licensed the survey. Fortunately, in this case, there is no territorial dispute.'

Cass tried to sound noncommittal. 'So Matt has moved on to another marine investigation, I assume.'

'He is still working off the African coast, but further north and on a different project.'

They were interrupted as Lili came running up to them. She was quite sturdily built, and Cass thought it unlikely that the little girl would grow to resemble her fine-boned mother. Lili's pink dress bore traces of grass stains and her hazel eyes brimmed with mischief. There was no ponytail today. Instead, her mop of curly hair had been secured with ribbons

114

in two bunches, immaculate an hour ago, less so now. She said a shy 'hello' to Cassandra, but obviously couldn't wait to get back to the other children.

As she skipped away, Cass said, 'Her colouring is so fair. She obviously takes after Istvan, your husband. Are they similar in personality too?'

Anna looked surprised out of all proportion. 'Istvan is not Lili's father!' Her face softened as she looked across to where Lili had started a game of hide-and-seek with several girls of the same age. 'Istvan loves her as his own daughter, and Lili loves him in return. It was a terrible time for us all when my first husband died. But perhaps, in some ways, it was easier for Lili that she was too young to realise her loss.'

'I'm so sorry! I didn't know.' Cass couldn't hide her astonishment. She'd never dreamed that tragedy lurked behind Anna's bright features.

'Why should you know, or even guess? We have built a happy family from the ruins, and in a few months Istvan and

I will be blessed with another child. We have waited a long time for this.' She patted her stomach, and Cass, for the first time, noticed an extra curve beneath the full skirt. As she murmured her congratulations, Anna's lips lifted in contentment, although her eyes were shadowed as she explained.

'My husband and Stephen were good friends. Because they worked together, Istvan and I already had much in common after the air crash. He, too, was distressed beyond words, but it was a long time before we came together.'

'Air crash?' Cass felt as though the ground was shifting beneath her feet. 'What do you mean?'

'They both worked — and of course Istvan still works — for a small commercial airline. The planes carry businessmen across Hungary to various conferences, but sometimes there are tourists, or people who wish to visit distant relatives with maximum ease.'

Memory was etching fresh lines on Anna's face. And then Cass realised they were always there, witness to the day when Anna's world had collapsed, but normally hidden beneath a lively interest in the person beside her.

As Anna paused, it was clear that she had forgotten the wedding and the sound of Magda's guests talking and laughing across the wide lawn. Instead, she had travelled to some other place, some other time. After a few moments she said, 'One day, by some freakish chance, a large bird flew into Stephen's path as he was landing.' Her serenity had gone, to be replaced by such raw grief that Cass was stunned. 'Fortunately he was alone and the airfield was quiet, so no one else died.' Anna's head was bowed and Cass could see how she was fighting back her tears. 'I was there, waiting for him. There were a few mechanics. We saw the crash, the fire. We could do nothing!'

'But Istvan does the same work! How can you bear it? To know he's doing the identical job that killed Stephen?' Cass heard her own voice rise in disbelief.

Anna's head lifted, her eyes warm with

sympathy as her own shadows moved away. 'I know you find this hard to understand, my dear. Matt told me about your fiancé's death. He explained — though there was no need to tell me, of all people — your fear of involvement with any man who works with danger.' She hesitated. 'Matthias has not known you long, but he was 'bowled over', as you say, the moment he met you. He loves you very much, but he is torn. He believes there is a chance that you could love him in return. But the work that he does has been his passion for years. To give up his career for you would destroy any chance of you making a good life together.'

'I understand. Of course I understand! But surely you must understand my feelings too? I can't face such a risk again!' Anna watched as, lost in despair, Cass pulled a leaf from the scarlet daisies that cascaded from a balcony above, and with agitated fingers tore it to shreds. 'I don't see how you can live with constant fear for Istvan, knowing how Stephen died!'

'It is not always easy,' Anna

acknowledged, closing her own fingers gently around Cass's hand. 'But it is better to have Istvan even for a short while than never to have him at all! My grandmother told me long ago that I must learn to cherish the golden moments, and that is what I do.' Her face was serious as she reminded Cass gently, 'If you turn your back when you find love, then what is the point of life anyway?'

They were interrupted as, strolling across the grass and holding Lili's hand, came Istvan. Anna introduced her husband to Cass and they talked for a short while, but the musicians began to play and Lili couldn't hide her impatience to join the dancing. She tugged Istvan's sleeve after a few minutes.

'Papa, can I go and dance?'

He looked down at the child. 'I shall have to think about it,' he teased. Frowning, he rubbed his cheek and pretended to think hard.

She tried to scowl, but then a gap-toothed beam broke through when, relenting, he grinned and told her to go. 'How can I concentrate on anything while I have a monkey prancing beside me?'

Cass watched the camaraderie between the two. No one would have guessed that Istvan wasn't the little girl's real father. And it was easy to see that Anna adored her second husband. They talked for a while until Cass smilingly told them to go and dance.

She looked at Istvan. 'Your wife tells me that you have to be up at the crack of dawn tomorrow.'

'Yes, but I shall not escape my duty on the terrace! Will you join us?' Istvan stood back, waiting for her to move forward. He was a nice man, she thought.

'In a while, maybe. But first I must have a word with Sophie.' The excuse worked, so then Cass had to make a point of finding Magda's cousin, who grabbed a glass of sparkling wine and thrust it into her hand. She was quickly caught up in the celebrations and even found herself dancing.

Before leaving the reception, Anna

came to Cass and handed her a slip of paper. 'This is the address and telephone number of the company that employs Matt. If you ever wish to contact him, they will help you. In these days of ship-to-shore communication and mobile phones, there is rarely a problem when he is abroad. The months have passed, but he has not changed his mind about you.' Leaning forward, she kissed Cass on one cheek, and then the other. 'I will not press you. I can only say that you should follow your heart. And then you will find those golden moments, as I have done.'

She had left Cass much to think about.

7

The long summer holiday arrived again. This year, Peter Sutherland and Liz had booked a villa with a swimming pool in the Languedoc region of southern France. They planned to share it with friends, driving in two or three cars. Would Cass like to come?

Cass jumped at the offer, relieved to fill time in a place far away from her flat, where the ghost of Matt wouldn't leave, occupying the big armchair, looking along her bookshelves, or strolling into the kitchen.

She already knew her travelling companions, and liked them. Reg, Liz's older brother, and Molly, his wife, were good company, as was Cass's bachelor uncle, David, and a married couple from the sports club that Cass had sometimes attended with Bryn. That seemed a long time ago now, and she found she could talk easily with them about various events, past and present. Bryn would always retain a special place in her heart, but the vacuum he'd left had grown smaller as her days opened to new interests and new friends.

The house party was, she supposed, what you might call a mixed bunch, but the journey through France was enjoyable. Apart from coffee-stops, there was an overnight hotel with coq au vin and a laden patisserie trolley. Cass found herself looking forward to the next two weeks. Hopefully it would give her some respite from thinking about Anna's words. Too often Cass had lain awake, turning them over and over in her mind. Was she like a little girl, crying for the moon, mourning a lost world, instead of cherishing the here and now?

At first, when the group had settled into the spacious, sun-kissed French gîte, she couldn't help marking the anniversary of that first trip to Hungary. From her bedroom window on the first morning, the view blurred: this was the day, one whole year ago, when she had bought her landscape painting from Matt. She could see clearly, as though he was standing beside her, the drawn lines of his face, witness to his recent illness; the dark hair touching the collar of his sky-blue shirt; and the intentness of his gaze as he gently tried to break down her reticence. Another morning she remembered that this was the day he'd taken her to Visegrád, and could see again the tumbled walls; hear his voice as he talked about the king whose summer palace it had been. Into her ears came the sound of gypsy music and the meal they'd eaten, before he'd kissed her under the moonlit sky and then inexplicably drawn back. But soon, here in France, the charm of the converted stone barn in the grounds of an ancient château, the vineyard-studded fields, and the vibrant, colourful local market held out enticing arms, drawing her into each new day.

At the start of their second week, they awoke to grey, scudding clouds and a drop in temperature. 'Climate change,' said Reg in mock gloom.

'Rubbish!' Liz slapped a plateful of bacon and eggs in front of him. 'Eat the nice English breakfast I've slaved to cook. By the time you've drunk your coffee, the sun will be out. Take my word for it!'

As she prophesied, the sky soon cleared. They'd gone to bed late after eating at a restaurant popular with local winegrowers. There was no set menu — you ate whatever madame was cooking that night — and it was superb. Various wines were recommended and tasted, the place was noisy and cheerful, the visitors welcome.

As the morning warmed, Peter and Liz drifted to the paved area that encircled an oval swimming pool, its blue water sparkling beneath the sun. One by one the others followed, though no one seemed inclined to swim as yet.

Cass made herself comfortable on a lounger and read for a while; but then, unaccountably restless, she asked her father if she could borrow his car. In the small town ten miles away she'd noticed amongst the market stalls several that sold second-hand books. Her knowledge of French was reasonable, although she couldn't tackle anything too obscure. There might be something interesting, though, and in any case, she would enjoy browsing. No one else wanted to go, so she set off alone.

She'd always loved the bustle, colour, and aromas that defined a French market, so the freedom to wander around the stalls at her own pace was a perfect way to spend the morning. It was hard to resist some of the antique bric-a-brac, but although her flat was ideal for one person, it was less so for the accumulation of pictures, ornaments and mementoes she could easily be tempted to buy. The market traders were cheerful and noisy as they shouted to each other and to people thronging the gangways. They hovered hopefully when Cass stopped to look at an old candlestick, a copper urn, and a blue pottery vase that held oil of lavender. Reluctantly she shook her head and passed them by.

The bookstalls were particularly hard

to ignore because there was such a huge variety of old and new, French and a dozen other languages. Making up her mind took time because, as a voracious reader, she tried to focus her attention on books that would be less easy to find when the holiday was over and she was back in England. Eventually, deciding on a few that hopefully shouldn't pose translation problems, Cass paid the stallholder. Casually dressed in scuffed jeans and a check shirt that had seen better days, he was young, bearded, and took her money with a grin. Laughing with him as he wished her luck, and pleased with her purchases, she moved away, stuffing them into her shoulder bag.

Breakfast had been a long time ago, she realised, and the hunger pangs were growing stronger, made worse as she passed great displays of cheese, cold meats and olives. People-watching was always fun, so she took time before deciding on a pavement café alongside the market square. It was crowded, and at first it seemed as though she'd have to find somewhere else. But then, noticing Cass, two women who were paying their bill beckoned and, smilingly appreciating her relief, wished her '*bon appetit!*'

Thanking them, she sat and decided this must be her lucky day. First the books, now an empty table; Dame Fortune ought to be waiting with one more throw of the dice. Her order came quite quickly, seafood salad with a small basket of crusty bread and a glass of dry white wine. It was delicious, followed by crème caramel and a leisurely coffee.

This was the most relaxed feeling she'd known for what seemed like ages. Fleetingly, Cass wished she could stay here for ever. But it was hard to push away the thoughts that crowded her mind, especially Anna's words as they parted in Szentendre. Without love, what was the purpose of life anyway?

It was early afternoon by the time she was ready to leave the café, and now the blue and yellow sunshade above her head wasn't needed. Dark clouds had returned, and soon came the first spots of rain. The crowds thinned, some taking shelter under the canvas awnings, whilst the stallholders hurried to cover their laden trestles.

Cass was halfway back to the gîte when the car started spluttering. Both she and her father had forgotten that last evening on their way home, the engine had coughed once or twice. Reg, a non-drinker, had been driving. He prided himself as something of a mechanic, so when he diagnosed a speck of dirt in the petrol, they'd believed him. Right now, Cass suspected it was more than a speck. More like a shovelful.

'Oh no! Please get me home! You can't do this to me!'

The engine died completely. The road was deserted, and had been since she'd left the market. Her father and Liz had deliberately chosen a holiday home in a remote area that Liz remembered from student years. The final approach meandered along a narrow track for about three miles and normally was a pleasure, emphasising the loneliness of their stay.

One side was bordered by thick woodland, a mixture of trees and overgrown shrubbery, and the other side formed the edge of a precipice. It fell steeply into a vast green valley where rows of vines stretched with mathematical precision into the distance. The sides were stony, the only access to flatter ground the few narrow vehicle tracks far below. There was no sign of life, not even a small building to be used by grape-pickers at harvest time.

Cass was wearing a T-shirt and jeans, and only a light sweatshirt that she'd flung on the back seat — a reflexive precaution from living in England, she'd thought, amused. Amused, that was, until she realised she'd left her mobile phone plugged into the charger that morning. It would still be sitting on the dressing table.

'I'm going to get wet, very wet indeed,' she said aloud. There was no point in sitting waiting for someone to come along. The track led only to the gîte and the château, where they'd been told the owners weren't expected until October.

Her father and the rest of the group wouldn't worry about her until early evening, so no one would come in search for several hours. In any case, she'd enjoy a walk, even a wet one.

The first mile was refreshing, almost easy. The rain was light, and underfoot the ground was dry, although she had to watch for potholes in the worn tarmac. But then the heavens opened and the wind strengthened. In seconds it began to tear through the trees, forcing branches to bend and casting showers of leaves. Above, any white clouds had drifted, hidden at first by pale grey, and then the grey developing into something closer to black. Shivering, Cass felt as though they were calling for her to reach out and touch them. Hurrying along the track, she was soon completely drenched.

A rumble of thunder came. Then came more — deafening, threatening, as the elements waged war. Forked lightning blazed the valley, jagged and awesome, as the sky split, unleashing its fury.

Cass stopped dead. Her first instinct

was to dive for shelter. There was cover on one side, a steep drop on the other. Already she was soaked, so it made sense to keep moving and get home fast.

'Lightning and trees don't mix! Keep walking.' At home, she often talked to herself, just for company. But she didn't feel alone. Nature was in charge: magnificent, awe-inspiring. And suddenly Cass wasn't scared. The rain lashed and, saturated, her clothes clung, but she wasn't cold. Her eyelashes were so wet, she could scarcely see. The precipice was perilously near. Was this the edge of the world? Wild, wonderful, and savage!

Was this how Bryn had felt — buoyant, a free spirit, fighting the rapids? Or on a jagged mountain? Was this how Matt felt when he dived into dark waters? Did they abandon themselves, feeling joy as they let go of safety? Cass had faced extreme weather with Bryn, but nothing like this, and never alone. This was the first time she'd known such solitude. And she loved it.

She should have been afraid. Unsparing

winds were ripping open her cocoon, the one she'd spun as a safeguard against the world when her mother died, the haven she'd strengthened when Bryn died. And again, the one she'd sheltered inside so that she could send Matt away.

Cass stood on the edge of the rocks overlooking the valley. Scalding tears and cleansing rain washed her uplifted face as, for the first time, she faced reality. It wasn't exactly a revelation; more an acceptance of the truth. Floundering in a vortex of grief as she lost first one and then another of those dear to her, she'd thrown up a barrier that allowed no incomers.

Truth was here, forcing open her consciousness. And truth told her that Nature didn't keep its power for the elements alone. It crept into the minds of humans, taunting, weaving its magic around their hearts and minds, like the song of the Lorelei. How could anyone resist the call?

It was time to leave the barren land and take the risk of living — and loving — again.

8

Cass didn't waste any more time. As soon as the holiday ended and she returned home, she took out the scrap of paper that Anna had passed to her at Magda's wedding. It gave the address and telephone number of Matt's company. When she rang, the switchboard operator gave more information than Cass could have hoped for.

'Mr. Benedek is due to attend a conference here tomorrow,' she said. 'If you let the reception desk know you're waiting, you might catch him before he goes to lunch. Otherwise, the secretary could ask him to ring you before he leaves London.'

Cass thanked her but left no message, merely saying that she would contact him later.

The company's head office was located in a central area of London. By eleven o'clock next morning, Cass was outside the building. She could see only one entrance, obviously the main one, with tall marble portals fronting a narrow street not far from Trafalgar Square. Concrete pavements and anonymous office blocks concentrated the heat of the late August day, and the crowded thoroughfares were alive with office workers and tourists in summer clothes.

Her spirits echoed the sunshine. For months since parting from Matt, she'd felt as though she had thrown away something that was precious, by being frightened to walk into the unknown. Today she was taking her first positive steps in several years, ever since Bryn's death, and it felt good.

For more than an hour, she sat in the window of a coffee bar which conveniently offered a view of the doorway through which Matt must emerge if he was attending the meeting. Suppose he hadn't come? Her nerves began to jangle, but quickly she scolded herself for being defeatist.

Eventually, when it seemed likely that

the conference would break for lunch, she went outside again, heart thumping. Was this a crazy thing to do? Supposing Matt had changed his mind about her? How embarrassing it would be! Then she recalled his steady gaze, his quiet voice, his warmth, and the sensitivity with which he'd accepted that she couldn't bear to share his life.

It helped, too, to remember Anna's words. Matt's friend, someone who knew him well, was convinced that he still loved Cass, even after so many months, and even though he thought the little English history teacher couldn't be part of his future.

No, Cass reassured herself, Matt wouldn't have changed. But she had! Her love for him was stronger than ever, and she could accept that his work was a vital part of his makeup. The big difference now was that she understood what drew him to search the oceans, despite their hidden dangers. If she sent him out of her life, she would lose so much that made it worth living. What was the point of half an existence? Yes, he'd often be thousands of miles away, but then he would come home to her. And she'd be waiting.

The heavy door opened and several men came out. One of them was Matt. Astonishment and swift delight lit his face. He took a long stride forward, hands held out in greeting. Then, obviously remembering how they had parted, he hesitated. Even so, the warmth in his eyes couldn't hide his feelings.

'Cassandra! This is a surprise! What brings you here?'

'Hello Matt!' Courage fled. Cass floundered, and then inspiration came. 'I'm on my way to the National Gallery. There's a special exhibition I'd like to see.' Oh heavens! Why had she said that? If he asked what the exhibition was about, she'd have no idea. There might not even be one.

He made no comment. Uneasily, she saw him raise an eyebrow, possibly registering the east-west direction of this street, whereas the National Gallery was to the north. His companions were talking casually as they waited in the background. Glancing over his shoulder, Matt told them to go ahead. 'I'll follow in a moment or two.'

They must have booked lunch in one of the big restaurants, Cass realised uncomfortably. There were lots in this area, servicing business meetings, and other more casual bars where already she could see tables filled with office workers.

'Don't let me delay you,' she said, although the last thing she wanted was for him to hurry off. She'd summoned up courage to tackle him this time, but wasn't sure that she could nerve herself to do it again. 'You're on your way to eat.'

Matt drew the corners of his mouth down. 'I would prefer to eat with you, if you are free, but my colleagues and I must discuss an important project over lunch. Our meal will be light, so there is no danger of us falling asleep when we return to the boardroom!'

His lopsided grin reminded Cass of the endearing humour she had known from him during those heady days in Szentendre. It brought to mind also her reason for being here. She took a deep breath. This was no time to be coy, or embarrassed. She was fighting for her future, his future, their future.

'Matt, I need to talk to you,' she said desperately, knowing she mustn't lose this chance. 'Anna encouraged me to contact you.'

'She was right!' His voice was deep. 'I had thought never to see you again.' Suddenly the accent of his homeland was there. He, too, was remembering. He paused, his eyes intent, as though memorizing every contour of her face. 'My world was grey without you.'

'Oh Matt! My world has been grey, too.' Cass blinked, feeling a roughness in her throat. She forced herself to go on, though all she wanted was to throw herself into his arms and cry. 'I've done a lot of thinking. But, more than that, I've learnt to understand.' Tremulously, she laughed, although she couldn't control her tears. 'I'll admit that I wish you'd be content with painting the Great Plain of Hungary! But that's part of the fool I've been, so afraid of life … the woman who's been wasting it!'

Cass realised that her hands were being held tightly and Matt had moved so close that she could feel his breath on her cheek. He glanced in the direction his colleagues had taken. They were entering a discreetly marked restaurant a hundred metres along the street.

'I must go now,' he said reluctantly. 'But I should be free by six o'clock. Could you meet me then?' His mouth quirked. 'Perhaps you could find a seat in the National Gallery when your feet demand a rest?'

A glance upwards told Cass that he'd seen through her excuse. Of course, the artist in him would have known about, and probably already visited, any current exhibition. Knowing her luck, it was probably a collection of structural engineering designs.

Sliding his hands up her arms, Matt lowered his dark head and brushed her lips with his own. 'I am so glad you came, my lovely Cassandra.'

'I'm glad too.' At last she could look at him, her clear grey eyes filled with a love that she knew there was no need to hide. 'I'll be here at six.'

She couldn't have described the paintings she saw that afternoon. Some were beautiful, some were brightly coloured, some she thought drab, some hideous. By the time she wandered into each spacious room of the gallery, she had forgotten the pictures she'd seen in the previous one. It was hard not to dance, to skip, to sing. He'd been happy to see her! There hadn't been time to explain her change of heart, and she needed to tell him how it had evolved. He would accept her word without that explanation, but she wanted everything between them to be open and honest.

London was full of tourists as usual, and today Cass enjoyed being one as well. Sunshine glittered in the fountains in Trafalgar Square and she sat for a while enjoying the spectacle. It seemed that everywhere she looked people were taking photos. Most were small family groups, many from the far east, their women in brilliantly coloured gowns, or others garbed in flowing black. Some tried to stand back far enough to capture a view of Nelson, lofty on his column. The massive bronze lions on their granite plinths reminded Cass of a male colleague whose shaggy leonine head topped a thickset body and big hands that he used like windmills to emphasise particular points, or draw a response from his hapless pupils.

Matt would make a good teacher, she mused. Intelligent, clearly spoken, a responsive listener, he would take the trouble to make lessons interesting.

Wind lifted fountain spray, sprinkling her face and bringing her back to earth. Water was going to ride high in her mind. If she wanted to enter Matt's world, she'd better get used to the idea that he would continue to sail the world's oceans and occasionally explore their murky depths. Stepping into dangerous waters wasn't a prospect she relished, but it was a price she would willingly pay.

At six o'clock she returned to the place where they had met earlier. Soon the great oak door opened, and Matt emerged with another man. With a casual word they parted, and Matt strode towards Cass. Reaching her, he lifted her hand to his lips, and then, careless of onlookers, bent his head to kiss her on the mouth.

'Cassandra.' His words were a caress. His eyes absorbed every part of her — fair hair, wide eyes, short straight nose, the firm chin that was softened by the hint of a dimple, and the mouth, still pink from his kiss. Today she was wearing a shift dress in lime-green cotton, with chunky jewellery, the first she'd owned, a present from Liz. Her black sandals were stylish, their heels a modest height, a concession to London's pavements and the gallery. In the mirror this morning, she had felt that she looked good, and Matt's expression said she was right.

It was early to eat, so he took her to a quiet bar overlooking the river. As always, it was dotted with shipping both small and fairly large: tugs, private motorboats, or crowded sight-seeing excursion boats. When Cass asked about his partner, Paul, Matt confirmed that their survey aboard the *Venus* had been completed and that Paul had recovered from his long hospital stay.

'The people we were working for are more than satisfied with our company's report.' He frowned, grim lines deepening beside his mouth. 'You'll remember I told you that a man called Ben Holmes headed our team. When the truth about Paul's 'accident' came to light, and the reason for it, he only narrowly escaped prosecution. In the end, the directors took his long service into consideration, plus the fact that he'd run into big financial trouble at home — his wife is the last of the 'big spenders' — which, of course, made him vulnerable to a bribe.' Matt was gazing across the water to where Tower Bridge had raised its central arc, but Cass realised he wasn't seeing it.

'Holmes had risked Paul's life, and that's something I find hard, and at present impossible, to forgive.' Sighing, he watched the white foam trailing a crowded pleasure boat as it made its way downstream. 'The man is not all bad,' he admitted reluctantly. 'His conscience ultimately led to a full confession. He was close to retirement, and so he left immediately, knowing he'd escaped lightly. He'll have to live with the fact that his greed might have resulted in Paul's death — murder, in fact, and that won't be easy.'

Silently they sat for a while, and slowly his expression relaxed. They didn't need to speak. That could come later. For now, it was enough to be together.

Matt had somehow found time from his meeting to reserve a table for dinner at a waterside restaurant, where soft background music and candle-lit tables created an intimate, relaxing atmosphere. It was an intoxicating experience, thought Cass, this time of getting to know each other, when both could talk without any of the old restraints — Matt without secrets; her without fear of being hurt.

They took time selecting their food, arguing amicably. Was it best to choose the main course first, and only then look at the page that listed the starters? Matt caught Cass taking a sly look at the list of desserts. She admitted she could never resist doing that. 'Just to make sure I leave enough space if there's something I absolutely love.'

'Like treacle tart and custard?'

'Or even better — chocolate fudge cake with cream!'

'I don't believe you, you mere slip of a girl!'

The meal was perfection, and they were happy to talk generally, touching lightly on Magda's wedding and Cass's holiday in France. It was only after they left the restaurant and started wandering along the Embankment that they spoke more seriously. Lights from the far bank of the Thames dappled dark waters, smooth without their daytime procession of barges and cruise boats. The constant low hum of traffic was muted, and the air was balmy. Life felt good, thought

Cass, especially with her hand securely in Matt's firm clasp.

It was time now to tell him how she had talked to her father, and to Anna.

'Dad felt that he'd wasted years after my mother died, years when she would've wanted him to pick up the threads of life again. He did it, at last, with Liz. They're well matched, and I can see how right she is for him.' Cass smiled, remembering how glad she'd been to watch them living, laughing and home-making together.

'And then I met Anna again at Magda's wedding. She knew, of course, that I'd sent you away.' Remorsefully, she glanced at his face, but it told her nothing. Drawing a deep breath, she went on, remembering how she'd been that evening in London, and regretting her actions. Understanding had been in his eyes as he'd listened, and he'd made no attempt to persuade her. She knew that despite his silence now, the grip of his hand was encouraging her to go on.

'I was astounded when Anna told me how she'd been widowed so young. Even though her husband died when his plane crashed, she'd had the strength to move on. Falling in love with Istvan, another pilot doing the same job with the same company, was the sort of courage that I have shrunk from. She was trying to help me, and she did. I'm happy that they're creating a home together with Lili. And soon, of course, there'll be a new baby.'

Matt was listening intently, still saying nothing. Cass paused, searching for words to explain that moment in France when the storm had seized her — buffeted, saturated, and rendered her at peace with the natural world; its force ... and its glory. As she tried to describe it, she felt again the wind and rain, and the fury.

'I revelled in the wildness, the freedom. I flew without wings.' His hand tightened around hers and she knew he recognised his own reaction to the elements. 'For the first time, I understood what makes people reach for the unknown. I couldn't help thinking of the Sirens perched on their rock, an irresistible force. And I can understand, too, how that world beckons you towards the sea and its mysteries.'

They walked in silence for several minutes. Matt's thoughts had taken him back to the evening in her flat when, without words, he'd accepted that Cass couldn't face the life he had to offer. He'd understood her feelings and respected them. This transformation in her feelings was wonderful, and yet it made him face a decision for which he had no answer. It wasn't simply a question of head versus heart, but something more complicated.

His head said that he'd be a fool to relinquish a career of which he was proud, and would provide a comfortable lifestyle for a wife and family. The real problem came from a heart that pulled him in opposite directions. Along one path lay work for which he'd undergone extensive training, work that he enjoyed and was unfailingly a source of interest and wonder. The other path led him to Cassandra, a woman he loved more than he'd ever thought it possible to love. He'd met his soulmate and longed to spend the rest of his life with her. But was it fair to

149

burden her with fear that, although the risk was relatively small, she might again know loss and grief?

At last he said slowly: 'Yes, I've heard the Siren's song, and so did Bryn. And now you've heard it for yourself. Admittedly, it can lead a man to his death, and I know that I must take care. But you, my love — can you live with the reality that sometimes my work involves risk? I won't pretend; there can be danger.'

'Can you live with the knowledge that I cross busy roads every day on my way to school?'

His answer was to swing her around into his arms and kiss her. He took his time over it, and when he eventually released her, Cass was speechless.

A clock chimed. 'I must take you home,' he said.

'Shall I see you tomorrow?' she asked, secure in the knowledge that she would.

'Tomorrow I leave for Africa.'

Shock punched her in the stomach. She couldn't hide a low, protesting gasp.

He drew her close, near to where a

jetty met the Embankment wall and they could see the lights of a late riverboat make its way silently upstream. His hands cupped her face. 'This is how it would be, Cassandra. No nine-to-five husband returning home to dinner each week.'

Cass had recovered. 'This is how it will be', she corrected him. Then, lightly, 'But after a while, there will be several more weeks when he's at home, getting under my feet twenty-four hours a day.'

'Exactly!'

9

The next few weeks were the happiest Cass could remember. She supposed that somehow she must have taught the school's education syllabus, marked essays, and kept order in class, but the days passed in a haze of sunshine. When she walked, her steps felt as light as thistledown, and her eyes were bright, acknowledging that life was good. Although she and Matt had made no concrete plans for the future, she knew they would be together. He telephoned her from the ship every few days, although he warned that sometimes the *Venus* would reach areas where reception was limited or nonexistent. Their conversations were brief, the line unclear; but despite the distance, Cass felt as though he was in the room with her, his love and warmth almost as tangible as the landscape she'd bought from him the first time they met in Szentendre. Titled 'The Great Plain of Hungary', it was a constant reminder of that day as it hung on the wall above her desk, retrieved from the cupboard where she'd once hidden it.

One evening Matt had good news: he should be home within ten days. The new survey was going well, and he'd been mainly engaged in computer analysis. The only diving he'd done was for fun, he said.

Cass was glad he didn't try to hide the fact that he'd been underwater, even deeply underwater. It meant he believed her assurance that she had come to terms with the occasional hazards of his job. She knew she'd be deceiving herself if she had no worries about his safety, but she knew also that she had faced her fears and could control them.

Before he rang off, Matt said they must make wedding plans. He couldn't see her mischievous eyes, but he could hear the lilt in her voice.

'Wedding? What wedding? I don't remember any proposal of marriage. Is this what they call 'taking a woman for granted'?'

'Oh dear heaven! Did I never ask you?'

She shook her head, and then, remembering he was several thousand miles away, said, 'No.'

'My darling Cass, I am sorry!' He sounded genuinely dismayed. 'It's just that …' Unusually, he struggled to find words. 'When we met again in London, it seemed so natural to be with you, as though it had been that way for years. And already I knew that we would stay together … for all time. Didn't you feel it too?'

'Yes,' she admitted, but then brutally added, 'I would still appreciate a formal proposal. I'm an old-fashioned lady, you know!'

'That's a relief! As an old-fashioned guy, it's the only species of woman that I can cope with!' His voice held a smile as he heaved an artificial sigh, loud enough to travel the sound waves. 'I suppose there's no escape.' His accent grew stronger in the way she had come to recognise at times. 'When I reach home, I will beg you to marry me.'

'On bended knee?'
'On bended knee.'

* * *

When he arrived at Cassandra's door ten days later, he pulled her into his arms and kissed her with a new urgency, as though the sight of her had lighted a touch-flame, one that had burnt softly from the moment they'd said goodbye. Cass wasn't slow to respond because she, too, had known a desperate need to be with him again. They'd had so few hours alone, and that final time had left so many unanswered questions. Before any wedding plans were made, what was in his mind? Were they going to live together? How would she feel if he suggested it?

Her arms tightened around his neck, sending a signal of the need she'd felt during these long weeks apart, and he wasn't slow to respond. She'd been forced to realise how differently she responded to Matt's lovemaking, compared with the way she had been with Bryn. With him, she had known tenderness, affection, but never the flame that threatened to engulf her when she felt the strength of Matt's lean, lithe body close to hers. Reluctantly, at last he released her and glanced at his watch.

'I'm late and you must be starving.' His voice was husky and she knew that he, too, was finding it hard to come back to the present. 'I booked a table for dinner at a very special Hungarian restaurant in town.' He drew her close once more, his lips brushing the curve of her cheek before he dropped a light kiss on the tip of her nose. 'It will remind you of Szentendre and give you fair warning that I am descended from warrior tribes. So beware!' She didn't need reminding. His dark hair and olive skin and the lean sculptured lines of his face betrayed his eastern ancestry, and so did the soft tones of his native language.

'Magyar horsemen thundering across the Great Plain, your namesake Matthias Corvinus and his army?' Cass arched an eyebrow and, when he nodded, went on: 'Wasn't he also a man of culture, who loved the arts and literature … ?' She kissed Matt, a kiss reciprocated so thoroughly that she struggled for breath as she whispered, 'I'm not afraid.'

'Come — we must leave, or I shall be tempted to stay.' His blue-grey eyes darkened as he looked down at the fair head tucked beneath his chin. 'And then we shall both starve.'

Their meal was wonderful. It was a fairly small restaurant, where dark-panelled walls and deep-red velvet curtains and chairs were softly illuminated by exquisite fluted glass table lamps. It was obvious that several of the other diners were known to the head waiter, who greeted them in what Cass recognised as the Hungarian tongue. Matt translated the menu for Cass, but then he, too, ordered their food in a language unfamiliar to her. Firstly they were served a delicious soup, followed by a main course that reminded her of their dinner on the way home from Visegrád, more than a year ago. With it they drank a dark red wine, mellow but strong enough for Cass to place her hand across the top of her glass when Matt leant to top it up.

This evening they were miles from Szentendre, and there were no gypsy violinists in colourful Hungarian costumes, but nevertheless, the atmosphere was the same. If Cass closed her eyes, it was easy to pretend she was there, and that not far away, the Great Plain was host to millions of beaming golden sunflowers, squat thatched farmhouses, long-horned cattle and horsemen in broad-brimmed black hats, carrying long stock whips.

For dessert, Matt insisted that she should find a tiny corner to try a pancake folded around hot cherries and served with cream. Eventually she leant back in her chair and sighed. 'That was complete and utter bliss!'

Between courses, and while they drank their coffee, Matt told her more about the project he had been working on, and life on board the *Venus*. His quarters were small but adequate, he said, and the food tended to be hearty rather than haute cuisine.

'The ship's captain and crew are sturdy fellows — they have to be — but they need energy. A sailor's life can be a hard one.' In answer to her questions, he explained that on his current project there were nine members of the survey team. A new hydrographic surveyor had, of course, replaced Ben Holmes, who had retired and was doubtless thanking his lucky stars that the company hadn't prosecuted him. Matt was there as a marine geologist, studying the composition of the ocean floor, and others were mainly involved with computer analysis of data retrieved from the depths. His former partner, Paul, had completely recovered from his diving ordeal, but was currently with another survey team and working off the west coast of Australia.

Amusement creasing his face, Matt listened to Cass's description of a new boy in her tutor group. 'He's a freckled, snub-nosed pot of mischief. Not a bad lad — just full of life.'

Watching the curve of her lips, he said,

'I think he has found a soft spot in your heart.'

'Or in my head!'

A second cup of coffee was brought personally by the head waiter, who obviously knew Matt well. The two of them launched into a conversation of which Cass didn't understand a word. Waving away their apologies, she assured them that after such a magnificent meal, she was happy to sit and relax while they talked.

Afterwards, they walked slowly through the streets beneath a sky that was studded with stars, particularly bright tonight in the crisp air. It wasn't too cold, though, to sit on a bench beside the water once they'd reached the park. During the day there would be people strolling along the paths; perhaps a few cyclists. Squirrels, playing on autumn flowerbeds, would perch on the low railings, glad to take nuts from friendly hands. Tonight only a few people lingered, mostly couples.

Matt's words were as deep and dark as the river. 'You told me I'd forgotten something important, and so I had.' Standing, he drew Cass to her feet and led her to where the wide pathway, empty now, overlooked a dark but glinting and magical River Thames. Catching her shoulders, he drew her close. His eyes were in shadow, but she knew they were warm as they traced the delicate lines of the face she lifted to him.

'I must tell you that from the moment you walked into Anna's courtyard in Szentendre, I have loved you. I didn't even know I had been waiting. But suddenly you were there!' His teeth glinted white in a smile as the soft breeze swayed the Embankment lights. 'I can't write poetry about your hair, your face, your figure, but one day I want to paint that portrait of you. And then you will see that every brushstroke is done with love.' Sliding his palms down her arms, he captured her hands. 'I would try to make you happy, Cassandra. Will you marry me?'

She didn't hesitate. 'I love you too, so very much. Of course I will!' Releasing her hands, she placed her palms on either side of his face, and leant closer until their breaths mingled. Half-laughing, she murmured, 'Especially as it was such a beautiful proposal!'

'In that case, will you wear this ring for me?'

Set in a fine band of gold, the sapphire was mounted in an antique setting. As Matt slid it onto her finger, she lifted her hand to see it catch the beam from a streetlamp behind where they stood. It fitted beautifully.

They walked on to where he had left the car which, he said, he found useful for his occasional trips to England. 'It's an expense that I could do without, but I like the freedom to visit colleagues and friends when I am here. And, of course, when we marry I shall have reason to be here constantly.'

As Cass opened the door of her flat and looked at him hesitantly, he followed, and closed it behind them.

'I think you know how much I am tempted to stay. But as I've told you before, I'm an old-fashioned guy. I want our wedding and everything about it to be special, my love.' The blue-grey eyes were dark again, but warm, and held the promise of a new beginning — not now, but soon.

Closing the door a few minutes later, Cass sighed. Her wedding day couldn't come soon enough, and then Matt would be with her. Still, a small voice whispered that he'd only be with her sometimes, and that there would be many lonely days and nights when he was at sea.

The following morning Matt returned and, after a late breakfast of scrambled eggs and coffee, they drove to his flat, fortunately only a few miles away. It occupied the top floor of a modern block overlooking a green, open area, and although it was less colourful than hers, it held books, paintings and memorabilia from his work overseas, enough to entertain Cass for hours.

She sat on the comfortable leather couch while he telephoned Anna to tell her about their engagement. Even from the far side of the room, Cass could hear her ecstatic reception of the news, and

Lili's high treble in the background asking to be bridesmaid. When Matt beckoned, she went to the phone and could hardly understand Anna, who was talking so fast, clearly delighted that Cass had taken those few steps into the unknown and would be part of Matt's life from now onwards.

Matt was chuckling when she eventually replaced the receiver. 'Anna is convinced she has played Cupid and that we owe her a very large bottle of champagne, or even an original Van Gogh!'

'She's right about the bottle and even the masterpiece,' said Cass as she came to slide her arms around his waist. He rested his cheek on her head as she said, 'I'd been such a coward. When she told me about her own suffering, I was ashamed that I'd hidden from life and love, whereas she'd found the courage to walk forward into the future. Even so, I might never have found the nerve to approach you without her encouragement.'

Magda, too, when Cass telephoned her flat in Budapest, was delighted, but wanted reassurance.

'Are you certain, my friend, that you can accept Matt's regular absences, the reality of his work? Often you will not know where he is or what he is doing. At such times, one's imagination can play cruel tricks.' Unusually hesitant, she went on, 'I would not want you to spend each day fearing that knock at the door, or dread that a phone call will tell you that some bad thing has occurred ...' Pausing, and knowing that Cass would understand her meaning, she added, '... again.'

It took some time to persuade her friend that whatever the future held, Cass wanted Matt to be part of her life. The Hungarian woman was a good friend, and right to be anxious, knowing how Cass had reacted to the loss of Bryn. He was still a sweet memory, but just that — a memory. At last Magda was persuaded that Cass had left fear behind and was ready to move forward.

'Then I suggest you buy a second home here in Hungary, so that we can see much more of each other!' She rang off after making Cass promise to keep her informed of every detail as the wedding was planned.

After two weeks, Matt would have to return to sea to complete this latest project in Africa. In the meantime, he worked at home occasionally, but mainly at his company headquarters. He sometimes managed to meet Cass when she left school at the end of her day, and they would spend an hour or more walking along the Embankment or in the many London green spaces before eating at small, intimate restaurants or bistros that one or both knew. Often Cass would cook a meal at her flat, while at other times they went to Matt's, where he guided her through the mysteries of Hungarian cuisine. Neither apartment, they agreed, would be suitable for married life, because one room would have to be set aside as a study for Matt, and Cass also needed a space in which she could prepare her lessons and concentrate on the ever-present essay-marking.

There was no need for a long

engagement, but perhaps flat-hunting could wait until Matt had some leave before starting his next expedition. While he was away this time, Cass would start visiting estate agents, so that when he came home she could suggest possible locations, and have an idea of prices and what might be available.

It seemed best not to look for a house until they were ready to start a family. It was Matt who first raised the subject.

'Have you decided how many children we might have?' he asked teasingly when she arrived at his flat one afternoon after, as she put it, 'The day to end all days! I was issuing detentions like snowflakes!'

Cass shook her head, although of course she had imagined how it might be — a boy and a girl would be lovely, though if another came along, well that would be lovely too. The thought of having children with him thrilled her. Seeing the soft pink rise in her face, he laughed a little and stroked her cheek with a gentle finger, but she knew that to Matt also, it was a new and awesome thought, a huge step forward into the unknown.

Peter Sutherland and Liz took to Matt instantly. Although Cass had never doubted that they would, all the same she felt it was the final blessing. She knew that both were happy to see her move from the shadows and into the light of a new and lasting love. Her father, particularly, couldn't hide his pleasure; although he had liked Bryn, she knew her parent had tried to conceal a few reservations.

'You get on well, but you're completely different,' he'd said one cloudy day when she'd returned home exhausted after an expedition with Bryn and a group of teenagers keen to gain caving experience for a longer, more difficult underground trip in a few weeks' time. 'Bryn wouldn't read a book unless you tied him to a tree. He'll be off white-water rafting, climbing or whatever, whereas you, my darling daughter, would happily stay at home and sit under that tree with the story he'd discarded!' Cass had laughingly shaken her head, but deep down, unacknowledged, was the shadow of suspicion that her father was right.

Christmas was different this year, because Matt was invited for the celebrations. Cass sometimes felt she must be dreaming. Last December, thanks to her father and Liz, she'd survived. This time she felt bubbles of anticipation as each day dawned and she knew she would be spending it with people she loved.

There were visitors, of course. Liz's brother, Reg, came with his wife. Cass's Uncle David came too. There were carols, and the midnight service, and on Christmas Day an enormous dinner with crackers, sparkling wine and at Liz's instigation, silly hats. Afterwards, they exchanged presents before relaxing around the sitting-room fire. Soon Liz and Reg started telling Matt about their French holiday and the different incidents which had made the journey there and back so enjoyable. Amusement came first, followed by roars of laughter when David, not a thin man, confessed to his unsuccessful courtship of Monique, a superb cook, who worked in the Tante Marie restaurant where they'd regularly eaten.

'For the first time in years, I felt I should think about getting married. She had a superb touch with coq au vin!' After an ill-fated engagement in his early twenties, David had shied away from romance. If occasionally he'd been tempted, it was invariably by a woman who would feed him well.

A few days after Christmas, Cass took Matt to meet Marion and her family. This year there was no snow and no sledging, but still there were hot soup and rolls when they came home after an expedition to Box Hill, a short car journey away. It was a place that both Cass and Marion knew well from school trips before exams, college and careers had taken them in different directions. They'd always kept in touch, and Cass was godparent to Archie, one of Marion's twins. He and Sue, his sister, updated Cass on their latest school reports, all the time begging her to change jobs and be their history teacher, instead of the dragon they had to endure. Laughingly, she assured them that she could be as dragon-like as anyone. 'You should have a word with some of my class!'

Marion's brother, Richard, joined them for supper, an enormous stew that Marion insisted she'd 'whisked up' early that morning. Richard had brought a friend, an attractive redhead he introduced as Polly. His disarming grin was in evidence as he confided quietly to Cass that he still thought occasionally of his previous girl-friend; and, though he was quite smitten with Polly, 'I'm taking it slowly this time!'

It had been a lovely day, thought Cass as they drove away from the house, with Matt promising to send the twins postcards from as many exotic places as he could manage. He'd fitted in so naturally with her family and friends, and made her world seem complete. How glad she was that they'd finally come together!

By the time Matt was due to return to the *Venus,* he and Cass had decided on a summer wedding. The long school hol-iday would allow time for a honeymoon, and also a chance to settle into new and larger accommodation before the new term started in September. Her father was delighted, as much by the fact that Matt had become an integral member of the family as by Cass's new happiness. Liz regularly came home from work so full of extravagant ideas for the wedding and reception venues that they all threatened to sit on her.

It was hard to smile when Matt had to leave for Africa again. Cass managed it, but knew he wasn't deceived. Concern shadowed his eyes as, holding her face between gentle hands, his searching look questioned, threatening to tear away her hard-won composure.

When he'd gone, the days seemed empty. Cass knew this was likely to be the pattern throughout his working life. He'd be away for several weeks but then return to England for the next few, working sometimes at home, sometimes at the London office, where, waiting outside with shaky courage, she'd once wondered how to say she loved him.

Soon after Easter, they found a

spacious ground-floor flat in a large nineteenth-century house, once part of a wealthy estate but now the London suburbs. It wasn't far from Cass's school, and Matt was pleased that a thirty-minute bus ride would take him to the heart of the city. Set in its own grounds and split into three self-contained flats, it was near the local heath and perfect for long weekend walks and picnics. The estate agent thought it should be available, and the transaction completed, quite quickly.

Time sped by. When Matt came home the following month, the only drawback for Cass was that instead of relaxing together, there were always decisions to be made. Not only about the move from their separate flats to the new larger one, but also a hundred and one arrangements for the wedding. This was made more complicated by the fact that several of Matt's relations and friends would come from Hungary, including Anna and Lili. If he was free, Istvan, Anna's husband, would accompany them. Magda and Zoltan said they wouldn't miss it for the world, but would make their own plans to stay with friends in England.

'Wedding costs and moving house. That's all I think about these days,' Cass complained. They were sitting at the table in Matt's flat, trying to reduce the potential guest list to a reasonable size. 'What I really want is to sit with you for hours talking about art, seismic surveys and strange sea creatures.'

The lines beside his eyes deepened as Matt gave a low chuckle. 'And so you shall, my love, once we escape from everyone and start our honeymoon.'

'Promise?' She shoved away her papers and came around the table to perch on his lap. Curving her hand around his neck, she gave it a gentle squeeze.

'Promise!'

10

A month before the wedding, Cass was forced to hold tightly onto Matt's promise. Her telephone rang as she rammed bread into the toaster one morning. The caller wouldn't be Matt, because the time difference meant that he'd be working. Surely it wasn't someone, yet again, sorting out problems with the new apartment, or the wedding?

Her days were packed solid and seemed likely to stay that way for the foreseeable future. They'd decided that it was best for Cass to remain in her own flat and not attempt to move until Matt came home. Once he returned, they could start work on the new apartment. There were a few changes they'd like to make, particularly with colour schemes in one or two rooms. After that, they'd need to make major decisions about which furniture to keep and which would have to go. Another problem was books. Both Cass and Matt's bookshelves were overflowing, and both insisted that every volume was either essential or too beloved to part with.

Marion had dropped heavy hints about her animal charity shop. 'You'll have too many chairs, too many plates, too many of everything,' she'd declared. 'And here I am, crying out for stuff to bring in a bit of cash!'

Yesterday school was chaotic, as it had been most days recently. End-of-year exams were almost over, but these inevitably turned the normal timetable upside down. As children poured from the classrooms, some were relieved, others loudly dismayed as they reread question papers and compared answers. Next would come sports day, and though the school was lucky enough to have a fair-sized playing field, most of the staff were involved in forward planning for the different events. Once that was done, everyone's hopes rested on a dry day.

For the older children, apprehension was setting in as they faced the prospect of leaving school altogether. Suddenly the big wide world that they'd longed for seemed scarily alien. To make matters worse, Amy Dunne, who taught English, had broken her leg last weekend, so the rest of the staff were obliged to cover for her although a supply teacher, even for this final stretch of the summer term, would be coming to ease the burden.

Cass guessed that she would have few, if any, quiet moments today. Next week there'd be a final fitting of her wedding dress, which was being made by one of Liz's friends. Cass had faith in her stepmother's sense of style, and her trust was rewarded when she had gone for the first try-on a week ago. The dress was beautiful, a classic design in ivory satin that would show Cass's petite figure to advantage. It had a boat-shaped neckline, and Liz had suggested, as the perfect finishing touch, a coronet of small cream-shaded roses with a short veil.

Lili would be the only bridesmaid. Cass had sent a pattern and some sprigged blue silk to Anna so the Szentendre dressmaker could measure the little girl and make the dress.

The telephone was insistent. Whoever was ringing didn't mean to give up in a hurry. Cramming a hasty mouthful of toast into her mouth, Cass frowned at the kitchen clock as she lifted the receiver.

Surprised, she heard Anna's voice. Midsummer was a busy time, with plenty of tourists wandering around her art courtyard in Szentendre, but hopefully no unexpected snags had cropped up. Anna hadn't wanted to close it while she came to the wedding, so her sister-in-law, who helped her occasionally, had offered to look after the 'shop' for a few days, and could call on another friend for extra help if necessary.

The call had nothing to do with the wedding. After a brief greeting, Anna said, 'I know you must be in a hurry to leave for work. But before you go, can you tell me when Matt will be in England? Or do you know when he might telephone you? I need to speak to him urgently. A matter has arisen concerning my father's estate, and Matt is the only other executor. I cannot go ahead without his agreement.'

Cass knew that Anna's father had died two years ago, her mother ten years previously. The father had been an enterprising businessman, and this meant that his executors were faced with a mass of paperwork as they wound up his two companies. It had been a long and time-consuming process. Even so, Cass knew Matt was pleased that Anna's father had entrusted him with the task when Stephen, her husband and former executor, was so tragically killed.

'I'm sorry, Anna.' Hurriedly Cass swallowed another morsel of toast. 'I haven't heard from Matt since the end of last week. His ship was moving into deeper waters, he said, but the line was so bad that we didn't talk for more than a minute or two.'

'I think I will telephone the secretary at his headquarters,' said Anna. 'She is sure to know how I might send him a message.'

'Before you open shop for the day,'

said Cass, 'tell me quickly, how are the children?'

Anna's baby had been born in November, a little boy whom they named Rudi after Istvan's father. She said that Lili was enchanted with her small brother, 'and is actually quite helpful, so it is good practice for when she marries and has a young family!' Although Istvan treated Lili as his own, Anna confided her guess that he must be happy to have a son who, as the years progressed, might show traces of the genes he had inherited from his father and grandfather.

They talked for only a short while longer. Anna spoke excellent English, although she hadn't entirely lost that textbook precision which made her sound more formal than intended. Lili was looking forward to coming to England, and thrilled at the prospect of being a bridesmaid for the first time.

'Rudi is a good baby, so we can bring him to the church. If, by chance, he becomes restless, I can take him outside for a while.' News from Szentendre was that the courtyard studio was busy with visitors, and Anna admitted that she enjoyed talking to them but wished they would spend more money.

'I can understand that for tourists who travel by air it is necessary to buy souvenirs that are small,' she said. 'But there are other visitors with cars, who have room for our bigger canvases.' Reluctantly she rang off, knowing that both she and Cass must get ready for work. As Cass salvaged her cold toast, she thought for the hundredth time how lucky she'd be to have Anna as a friend for the rest of their lives.

Plunging into the school day, she scarcely had time to think about the reason for the call. But Anna telephoned again, late that evening.

'Cass, I have no wish to be alarmist, but I think it right to tell you.' She stopped.

'Tell me what?' Cass felt a finger of unease touch her spine. Anna was by nature a bubbly person, but tonight her voice held none of its usual lilt, and her attractive accent was more pronounced than it had been earlier.

'I telephoned Matt's company this morning. The secretary said she would need to speak to her employer and would ring me later. I heard nothing until an hour ago.'

'Is there a problem?' Cass heard her own question, sharp.

'There may be.' Anna couldn't hide her concern. 'They told me that they last heard from the *Venus* as it approached an area where there has since been a severe tropical storm. The ship is beyond the radar network and has vanished from the screens. There is also a satellite failure, which means that no radio communication is possible.'

'But the *Venus* can't just disappear!' Cass couldn't even contemplate such an idea.

'It is not impossible.'

'For goodness' sake, Anna, you're trying to scare me!'

'I would never do such a dreadful thing, my dear. But I felt it important to warn you. There may be trouble. Not bad trouble, of course!' The Hungarian woman didn't sound convinced, even though she tried to move on to lighter matters.

Next morning, after a restless night when she'd tried without success to laugh at her fears, Cass telephoned Matt's headquarters. There was still no news, but the secretary assured her that satellite breakdown happened every so often, and they could only wait for it to recover.

By the end of the following day, without news either from Matt or his employers, Cass's nerves felt as though they'd been through a paper shredder. Messages weren't enough. She'd got to find out more, directly from the company. Thank goodness the supply teacher who would cover Amy's classes had arrived, so that evening Cass rang Lyn Procter, her headmistress and friend. Lyn didn't hesitate.

'I've got the timetable here because I'm doing a catch-up job at home — a quiet spot on my personal planet,' she said comfortably. Her greying hair would have escaped from its casual knot and her spectacles would be lodged on the end of her nose. Cass heard her shuffling papers, which rarely seemed to be in order, although since her arrival three years ago the school's achievement record had soared. 'I see you've got a session with Class Eight tomorrow afternoon. As far as exams go, they've mostly finished, so you'd probably let them do private revision for the few language orals on Monday. Why don't I cover for you while you buzz into town? You'll feel better if you talk eyeball to eyeball with someone in authority.'

Cass detected a smile in her friend's voice as Lyn confided: 'You'll be doing me a good turn. It's a rare treat to escape my office, not to mention calls from stroppy mums. If little Johnny's been downgraded, there's a darned good reason for it.' Her voice lowered, but Cass didn't believe a word as she declared, 'Applying for a headship was madness. Give me the classroom and runny noses any day!'

Cass was laughing as she thanked Lyn, but her face was sober while she sat in the offices of the marine survey company next afternoon. As she'd feared, there was no fresh information, but Matt's immediate supervisor couldn't hide the fact that they were concerned. Shaking her hand, he introduced himself as Graham Stanthorpe, and led Cass to an office which might have seemed larger had the walls and every available surface not been covered in maps and charts. A thickset man nearing sixty, his eyes were shrewd as, waving his visitor to a chair, he sat facing her across a large mahogany desk. Realising after a moment or two that she was sitting bolt upright, her right hand nervously twisting her engagement ring, Cass tried to hide her tension. She obviously didn't succeed; his face was sympathetic as he glanced at her restless fingers.

From his sombre expression, even before he spoke she sensed that he had little news to offer. His desk was so covered with papers that it seemed unlikely he'd ever find anything. But he did, pulling towards him what looked like a recent fax message. Whatever it said didn't please him, even at this second reading. His mouth tightened, and she had a feeling he was searching for words. After a moment, he sighed and looked at her.

'I'm afraid there's little I can tell you at this point, Miss Sutherland. We're as much in the dark as you. I won't insult your intelligence by pretending that all's well and we've no concerns. Of course we have — but stress is a major component of nautical life. There will always be problems, but … ' He hesitated. ' … we get through them.'

'You stopped short of saying 'We survive them,' interrupted Cass. 'Because you don't always — do you?'

He looked taken aback by the sudden attack. She'd appeared small, almost fragile, in her blue linen suit, and dwarfed by the high-backed chair in which she sat. 'Surely you must have some inkling of what might have happened!' she persisted.

'We know the *Venus* hit a bad storm, but since then we've lost all contact,' he said. 'Undoubtedly they would have been tossed around, despite stabilisers, so their engineers will be working on damaged equipment. And,' he added, anticipating her next question, 'the Indian Ocean's a vast expanse of water. Sometimes, I'm afraid, satellite and radar lose track of what's going on there.'

'Then why hasn't the *Venus* made its way back to base?' demanded Cass. 'Even if they'd lost every single aid to navigation,' she pressed on, though she knew she was grasping at straws, 'they could find their way by the stars!'

He smiled faintly, acknowledging her search for answers. 'As I said, they hit a storm. We don't appreciate their disappearance anymore than you do, temporary though it'll turn out to be.' Like Cass, he seemed to be trawling for reasons, although his next comment brought a new and unwelcome element into play. 'We're inclined to rule out piracy, because the *Venus* was in touch

187

with us until it moved into deeper waters, and the pirate ships aren't normally keen to venture that far.'

'Piracy?' Cass's cheeks blanched. Surely he was joking! If so, then it wasn't the least bit funny. Her mouth dried as she struggled to absorb what he'd said. But one look at his expression warned her that Stanthorpe was serious. His grey suit and red silk tie were formal, but he didn't look like an office person, she thought wildly. And it didn't seem likely that he'd ever pored over computer data in a ship's cramped cabin. So how could he have any idea of what Matt was up against? Solidly built, with a ruddy complexion and cropped grey hair, he had an air of the wide-open spaces. Perhaps he sailed a yacht. He could have played the part of a grizzled sea captain in some Hollywood film.

Across the desk, he didn't seem to notice her struggle to keep calm. He nodded as though piracy was an everyday occurrence for the company's vessels.

'You'll have heard of it through the

media. A few years ago it began escalating, but things have improved quite a bit, with international navies patrolling the ocean. All the same, you'll know, of course, that there are still too many incidents where pirates seize ships and demand huge ransoms.'

He picked up a paperweight in the form of a ship's wheel and started fiddling with it — glad, Cass suspected, of a reason to avoid facing her directly. But then he looked up suddenly. Clearly uncomfortable as he registered the stricken look in her grey eyes, he tried to soften the effect of what he'd been saying, probably wishing he'd had more tact than to introduce the subject.

'They're not all the swashbuckling characters you see at the cinema.' A faint smile was meant to lighten the atmosphere, but she couldn't respond. 'The problem started originally with the African fishermen. They'd had the sea to themselves, and vital fish stocks, enough to feed their families. Then suddenly foreign vessels started moving into their waters, reaping the harvest with their great nets and leaving them desperate. By threatening, even capturing foreign boats, they probably hoped to scare them off and put an end to what they saw as poaching. Unfortunately, the whole thing's progressed since then, and nowadays you've got the big overlords taking control. They send — ' He grimaced. ' — occasionally force, local men to do the dirty work of boarding and capturing. After that, the bosses demand a ransom, most of it to line their own pockets.'

The door opened and a secretary entered with a tray of coffee. Stanthorpe took one after she had placed another near to Cass. He offered the sugar bowl, ladling two generous spoonfuls into his own cup when she shook her head.

Cass sipped her drink, almost without realising. She was recalling media reports of ships being held for weeks, and others, with their crew, still lost. Instinctively she closed her mind to Matt's vessel being intercepted. All the same, she heard herself wanting to know more. 'The *Venus* was heading further out to sea, Matt told me. Pirates wouldn't have large enough boats for that. Surely they only attack nearer the coast?'

He shook his head. 'They use captured vessels as a 'mother ship', get out to sea and then send 'the workers' off in small, fast skiffs.' Realising that Cass was looking increasingly troubled, he made an effort to lighten his tone. 'We mustn't be negative, Miss Sutherland. Satellite malfunction is the most likely explanation for loss of communication with your fiancé's ship.'

'What about the storm?' Cass persisted. 'What about shipwreck? A tropical storm could easily sink a ship!' For one crazy moment it seemed even that would be better than pirates. She shook her head. Surely she was going mad!

'Tropical storms have a lot to answer for,' Stanthorpe said vaguely, obviously not wanting to be pinned down. 'For the present, I suggest you accept that the problem rests with the communication system.' Then, to her dismay, he couldn't resist a final, cautionary comment. 'It's just that we must consider all possibilities.'

Reaching the door as she left, Cass turned and looked up at Stanthorpe, who was close behind her. 'You will let me know the moment you have any news, whether good or bad, won't you?'

It was clear that he couldn't say no. Petite, and yet with a steely strength that warned she wouldn't be fobbed off with a noncommittal response, he found himself promising to keep her informed. Closing the door behind her, for an instant he envied Matt Benedek. This was the sort of woman who'd always be there, backing up her man.

If Matt's boss had been hoping to calm her, he hadn't succeeded, thought Cass as she caught the bus that would take her home. When she telephoned Anna that evening, they tried to raise each other's spirits, but she could tell that the other woman, too, was increasingly anxious.

'Matt does not need to telephone me often,' Anna said, 'but I know how he would want to be in touch with you whenever possible. It would be reassuring to hear positive news soon.'

They exchanged a few more words, but neither was in a mood to talk, so it wasn't long before Cass put down the receiver. Hugging her arms around herself for comfort, she looked at the armchair where he had so often sat. She could almost see him there now, dark hair untidy, long fingers turning the pages of a book, sometimes raising his eyes to where Cass was across the room, equally occupied.

Her heart was crying.

Where, oh where, was Matt?

11

Several thousand miles away, Matt was wondering the same. It had been a violent, even terrifying few days, when tropical skies and seas joined forces to brew a storm that was rare in its severity. As it approached, dark, low-hanging clouds had spread rapidly, hiding the blue. Streaked with red and orange, intensifying in colour, each ominous cluster soon took on the form of some malevolent fireball. And then, directly above the ship, splitting open, they released a tumult of noise and flame above a sea that was as black as the cauldrons of hell. Venomous, churning waves threatened to overturn the vessel and everyone on board.

Normally a good sailor, Matt had eventually sought his bunk, and several others succumbed even earlier. Despite stabilisers, the ship was no match for the forces of Nature, and the survey team and crew could do little but guard against being swept overboard.

At last, no longer buffeted by those mountainous seas, the *Venus* was still in trouble because the bridge had been badly hit. Fortunately, most of the hydrographic survey's lab space was situated on the mess deck, which escaped major damage; but the bridge held other vital equipment and echo sounders.

It hadn't helped that the storm coincided with an engine problem. The engineers were below deck, working on it now.

Worse was the captain's opinion that the *Venus* had been driven seriously off course. Not a problem in the normal calendar of marine life, but it could become one without full engine power or navigation aids.

'Could be we're too far north-west now, somewhere in the Somali basin.' Captain Evans, reliable and a good friend of the team, scanned the horizon with eyes which, as he sometimes put it, had 'seen more than their fair share' of hazards across the years. 'I don't say we're near to touching the Carlsberg ridge, but I'd sooner we got back down south.'

Dawson, the first officer, came from the bridge, where broken windows and snapped timbers evidenced the heavy rains and furious winds that had wreaked havoc. 'Not a glimmer from the radio, sir,' he said,' but they'll locate us soon enough I daresay.'

Evans grunted. 'Soon enough for them. Hope it's soon enough for us!' Muttering, almost to himself, he added, 'I don't mind telling you, I'll be glad to get away from here.'

Matt looked at him keenly. Their captain was a bluff, down-to-earth man with years of service at sea, and not prone to fancies. They'd weathered the storm, and his ship hadn't suffered irreversible damage, but he was uneasy. Matt held his tongue, but a quick exchange of glances warned that the first officer shared his feelings. It would be wise to get away from here.

'Better get some food inside us.' Dawson's grin was wry. 'Those who can face it!'

Matt followed him down to the mess deck, where the cooks had managed to put together a passable meal for the first sitting of crew members, about twenty in all. Of the nine members of the survey team, only he and three others were eating. Matt wouldn't have minded Paul's company right now; his solid common sense and ability to face troubles with realism, but with optimism too, invariably lightened tricky situations. And it looked as though this was one of them.

Although Matt had faith in the ship and its captain, through the worst of the storm he had fleetingly thought how Cass would believe all her worst fears had been realised if he — and everyone else on board — had died. Closing his mind to this, he wondered what lay behind Dawson's frown as the first officer sat across the table and speared a chunk of meat from what turned out to be a surprisingly appetising stew. The others had finished eating, so only the two of them occupied the long benches.

Dawson caught the expression in Matt's eyes. 'You're thinking the captain's worried. And not about storm damage.'

'Yes. We're further from help than he'd like us to be.'

'Correct. Let's cross our fingers and hope no one nasty —' He grimaced and drew a knifelike finger across his throat. '— spots us.'

'I know pirates are venturing into deeper waters nowadays.' Matt shot the other man a keen glance. 'D'you think we're at risk?'

'Could be. We know they're using captured vessels as mother ships to roam the regular shipping routes or look for someone like us. Once they spot likely prey, they'll launch a high-speed skiff to do the dirty work. The things appear from out of the blue and attack. It'll be wise to put extra watch on deck till we get out of here.' He grunted and attacked his meal with the sort of energy that made Matt suspect it wise to do the same. There was a long night ahead of them.

The *Venus* was unarmed, orders given

before leaving Mombasa that in the event of raiders, no resistance was to be offered. Evans repeated the order thirty minutes later, having gathered the crew and survey team on deck. After a quick briefing, he stressed the advice given by the port authorities.

'Basically, it's this. You're a long time dead, so if we're intercepted, make sure you do what these guys tell you. It gives everyone their best chance to get us and the ship back home again.'

Matt knew they were all prepared and mostly battle-hardened, apart from one or two younger crew members. Of those on board, he was mainly concerned about Dave, a teenage apprentice on his first marine survey job. Level-headed and a keen worker, this wasn't the sort of introduction anyone would wish on a newcomer.

Night came and was quiet, although Matt found himself tossing restlessly in his bunk. Constantly Cass was on his mind, his lovely wisp of a girl — no, a woman, for she was all of that and more, he thought, remembering the times when he'd found it hard to release her from his hold and say goodnight. By now she would know that the *Venus* had been caught in the storm. They'd talked about such possibilities, and of short lapses of time when there would be no news of him. But time was stretching out now. How would she be feeling about a complete lack of news? She would contact headquarters and Graham Stanthorpe, but he'd be as much in the dark as anyone.

Morning came and he'd snatched no more than a couple of hours' sleep. The ship's klaxon blasted. Startled, he jerked out of his bunk and threw on last night's clothes.

The breaking dawn, streaking the sky with pale orange and red, revealed the outline of another vessel, much the same size as the *Venus,* perhaps a kilometre distant.

The captain was standing by the bow, binoculars raised. 'I don't like it,' he said heavily. 'Seems we might have visitors.

But they won't be coming for tea and cakes!'

He turned to face those of the crew who were on deck. Matt and Rex, who was his opposite number on the project this time, and the survey technicians, moved closer to hear him.

'We don't want heroics,' Evans reminded them grimly. 'So keep your heads down and your mouths shut.'

Just then the engines spluttered into life. Too late.

In the dark mist of early dawn, a small skiff had reached them and tucked itself out of sight beneath the stern. A ladder had quietly been hooked onto the ship's rail, and the first pirate swung his leg onto the deck. Thin as a telegraph pole, swarthy and bearded, a red bandanna was knotted around his head. A black T-shirt and ragged canvas trousers with scuffed canvas shoes completed the outfit. One good punch would have sent him flying, but it was the necklace of ammunition, and even more strung around his waist, plus the Kalashnikov in his hands, that stopped them dead.

There was no chance to grab him. A deck-hand came too close. One swift thrust with the weapon and he sprawled unconscious.

Already two more pirates had climbed over the side, leaving a fourth in the skiff. One leapt up the steel steps to the bridge, returning in less than a minute. He raised his hands in a gesture meant to describe storm destruction. Their leader snapped a few words at him and his fellow, both heavily armed. They disappeared into the lower reaches of the ship.

The leader then stepped forward until only a couple of paces stretched between him and the captain. 'Start engines.' He pointed to where now, as the sun rose, they could clearly see the larger vessel waiting in the distance. He pointed to it. 'That way.'

Evans shook his head. 'Engine problem. Why d'you think we're not moving?'

There was no response. The man was African, almost certainly a Somali, but there was a toughness about his face and his stance that warned he was no ordinary fisherman. They would need to take care.

Dawson, standing near Matt, stepped forward. The gun swung menacingly. He stopped. 'Can you speak English?'

A grunt indicated yes.

'This ship is no use to you. We carry no cargo. No food. No oil. No medical supplies.'

An interruption came as the two men who had gone below deck returned, shoving before them Sparks, the foreman who'd been working on the engine. Short and stocky, his expression was belligerent as he stood with his feet spread apart, steadying himself when they dropped their hold. Hands tucked in the pockets of his bulky overalls, he looked at Evans.

'Cap'n, sir, this man seems a bit annoyed that we can't get the *Venus* moving.'

Evans faced the pirate leader. His tone was uncompromising, his shoulders straight, his eyes steely. A thickset man, he looked every inch the master of the *Venus*. 'I suggest you get back to your own ship,' he said uncompromisingly.

'Take any of our equipment that's of use. And then leave us to sink.'

12

Wearily, Cassandra closed the programme on her computer. Marking exercise books with a red biro was hard work, and she still did a lot of that. Today's world with its inevitable technology, however, wasn't quite as simple as people professed it to be. Not when it came to monitoring and assessing school assignments, anyway. Her back was aching, her eyes were aching, and oh how she needed another coffee! Her throat was dry, which could be the first warning of a cold. There were plenty going around school this week. That was the last thing she needed — a bug to drag her down almost as much as her dreary thoughts.

There was still no word of or from Matt, and it was increasingly hard to hold on to her determination to stay positive.

Early that evening, the phone rang. It

was Graham Stanthorpe. 'Are you alone, Miss Sutherland?'

As she said yes, her heart began to race. Already she knew he had no news that was good.

He said, 'I'll come straight to the point. But I must stress that you mustn't repeat this conversation to anyone. Anyone at all. It's essential that the media don't get hold of what I'm about to tell you.'

Cass could scarcely whisper, 'I promise.' Then, hardly daring to breathe, she asked, 'Have you found the *Venus*?'

'Yes. But we have a situation, I'm afraid.'

'A situation?'

His sigh came down the line. ''Fraid so. As I told you, there are international navy vessels patrolling, hopefully scaring away any pirate vessels with big ideas. A Dutch ship has been in touch with us, having sighted the *Venus*. They're having to stand off because it's in pirate hands.'

Cass felt her knees give way and she sank onto the carpet, dimly registering the need to keep calm. 'What can be done?' she whispered.

Stanthorpe hesitated. 'Hopefully they can negotiate. At all costs, we want to avoid a hostage stand-off.' Obviously regretting his promise to relay any news he received, he brushed aside further talk, only reiterating the need to keep silent.

Somehow Cass managed to exchange a few final sentences with him, thank him for keeping her informed, and promise that her lips were sealed, for the sake of Matt and his companions on board the *Venus*.

That night there was no question of sleep.

* * *

It seemed ludicrous that the next day, Saturday, Cass must wash her hair, wear one of her newest summer dresses, make her face up particularly carefully and leave the flat, braced to face Edna Weston's sharp eyes.

Bryn's mother had written a few weeks

ago to say that she was travelling to England in order to sell her old home. For the past two years she had rented it out through an agency, expecting only to holiday for a few months with her younger sister Joy in Australia. Normally Cass would have been delighted to see again the woman who had been like a mother to her for so long, but today was different. For the safety of everyone on board, she dared not breathe a word about the *Venus* and what was happening far away in the Indian Ocean.

When Cass had rather diffidently sent a letter with the news of her engagement to Matt, Mrs. Weston had immediately written a warm response. There was no doubt that she completely approved. 'I'm more than happy for you, my dear,' the older woman had written. 'And I have news of my own, but I shall be coming to England soon and I'll tell you then.'

When Cass reached the hotel near to the street where once both the Sutherland and Weston families had lived, her first reaction, after a warm hug, was complete surprise. Bryn's mother was much the same height as Cass, and not plump but 'well-rounded', as she put it. In past years she'd always favoured casual dress, often in soft shades of green or beige. Today, however, her linen suit was cherry red, with a crisp white blouse and high-heeled strappy black sandals, which had the effect of turning her into a quietly sophisticated woman. Gone was the neatly braided hair with tell-tale wisps of grey brushing each ear. Instead, every hint of the passing years had vanished, and short, light-brown curls framed a face that even wore a touch of eyeshadow.

'You look wonderful!' said Cass, impulsively hugging her again. 'Australia obviously suits you!'

'That's for sure, my dear. And I'm going to tell you all about it, so I hope you've put on your listening ears!'

Before going to lunch, Mrs. Weston suggested they should sit in the comfortable lounge and 'catch up over a cup of coffee'. Despite Cass's hard-concealed feeling of wretchedness and worry about

Matt, she couldn't help smiling at the familiar phrase. It took her back to her teen years — the shared memories, and the ever-present company and comfort of Bryn and his mother after losing her own.

Mrs. Weston's face registered a certain amount of disquiet as she looked at Cass across the low table. 'You're looking a mite peaky, I must say,' she commented. 'Is everything all right with your father ... and Liz ... and how is your fiancé?' Delicately she probed, but the only answer Cass could give to the woman who knew her so well was to force a cough, snuffle slightly, and blame her appearance on what she described as 'school-bred germs' which threatened to turn into a full-blown cold very soon. She wasn't sure that her companion was convinced, but it was the best she could do, no matter how tempting it was to pour out the despair she'd felt after Graham Stanthorpe's call. For Matt's sake, for the sake of everyone on board the *Venus,* she must be silent.

It was a relief when, having poured the coffee, her companion leant back and, despite her newfound elegance, automatically straightened the fold of a curtain beside the window where they sat. For a moment her expression held a trace of embarrassment, but then she smiled after joking about 'once a housewife, always a housewife' — viewing the orderly curtains with satisfaction, all the same.

'I'm getting married,' she told a stunned Cass. 'His name is Ken, and he's an old friend of my sister and brother-in-law. His wife ran off with a salesman years ago,' she explained, expressively raising her eyebrows, 'and he's fought shy of women since then. He came to dinner one night, and we got talking about cricket because he's an enthusiast — well, what do you expect, living in Australia? When I told him I always watched it on TV and had been to the 'real thing' at Lord's and the Oval, he invited me to join him next time he went to a match.' Her grin was unashamedly youthful, bearing witness to the increasing numbers who said that life began at sixty.

Cass knew she must show pleasure,

but worried that the woman who knew her so well would read an element of concern in her eyes. This would be such a completely new existence — far from 'home' in England, and with a husband after years of widowhood when she could do as she wished. Mrs. Weston read those thoughts and hastened to reassure her.

'I feel very comfortable in Australia, and of course having Joy there introducing me to her way of life and her friends has made all the difference. As for marriage, well I've spent enough time with Ken to feel that we'd get along very well together.' She chuckled. 'It's not what you'd call love's young dream, of course, but there's a lot to be said for a more mature sort of love — as long as you still get that tingle of excitement when you see each other!'

As Cass murmured her congratulations, Mrs. Weston leant forward and caught her hand. 'I'm so glad you've found someone, too, my love.' The lines on her face deepened, making her again the motherly figure who had always been there for Cass. Her voice lowered. 'I know how much Bryn meant to you, but yours was a young love, and who's to say how time would have dealt with the pair of you? There was Bryn, my lovely son, always stretching for the moon, no matter what the danger; and there was you, gamely tucking in behind, ever loyal, secretly wanting to sit and get on with your studies!'

As they both laughed, Cass felt able to relax in the knowledge that, like her father, even Bryn's mother had secret reservations about how their future as a couple might have played out.

Mrs. Weston said she was planning to visit the estate agent the next day, and that there was a prospective buyer who had already approved a survey and was keen to go ahead as soon as possible. Her tenants had moved out of the house a few weeks ago, so there only remained the final paperwork.

'And then I'm off back to Australia and my lovely Ken, ready for an October wedding.' Her unconcealed excitement was a ray of sunshine, and despite the fog of winter grey that smothered Cass's heart, she could only feel happy for her friend.

'We'll have a spare bedroom,' she was informed as they parted after a long, slow lunch, 'so Ken and I shall expect you and Matt to visit us before you start a family — and then bring them along with you as soon as they're old enough!'

13

By dawn the next day, Cass was aware that the sore throat which had been lurking for the past forty-eight hours was turning into a full-blown cold. Her eyes were burning; the dull headache she'd suffered since yesterday, even when she was with Edna Weston, was a raging pain in her temples; and she couldn't get warm. It was probably best to make a hot drink, swallow some painkillers, go back to bed, and try to sleep for a couple of hours.

A fitful doze only left her feeling it was too much effort to lift her head from the pillow. Thank goodness it was Sunday, so she could spend the day alone.

'There's no point in spreading my germs,' she croaked when Peter Sutherland rang just before he and Liz went to the tennis club for Sunday lunch. He wanted to know if there was news of

Matt. It was desperately hard not to tell him about Graham Stanthorpe's phone call. She trusted her father implicitly, but Liz would quickly pick up any extra concern on his face. Liz was wonderful, but with such an effervescent personality, there was just the faintest chance that she might let something slip to one of her friends. It was too great a risk.

Peter had already agreed that his daughter's visit to the survey company headquarters was the best way to gather news, even snippets, that would ease her mind. Reassuringly, he'd discounted Graham Stanthorpe's comments about piracy while she was in his office; though after replacing the receiver, he'd turned an anxious face to Liz. She'd tried to laugh away his fears.

'Darling, you've caught me watching *Pirates of the Caribbean* too many times, but it's only because I've a passion for Johnny Depp! I'll bet you a dinner at Al Forno's that this man Stanthorpe had the right answer. The *Venus* isn't a particularly new ship, but it's tough. You'll see

— it's just a communication foul-up.'

All the same, Peter wasn't deceived by his daughter's casual tone this morning as she said there was still no fresh news. Even if she dared tell him the truth, there was no point in worrying him even more.

'There's nothing I can do about Matt except wait,' she said. 'So it's best to dose myself up and sleep my germs off in bed.'

'Sleep' wasn't the right word. As Cass tossed and turned against the pillows, her thoughts couldn't stop revolving around Matt. Where was he? Was he safe?

Then, strangely, filtering into those worries, drifted visions of Bryn. He'd been such an important part of her childhood and teenage years. Cass pictured him firstly as an easy-going, sport-loving boy, and then as a young man with his head full of dreams. Eventually, thanks to his aunt's legacy, he'd been able to realise those dreams and earn a living from the outdoor activities he loved. Cass, his faithful follower, had been happy for him, with the fearlessness of youth.

At some point she fell into a heavy

sleep. And then the nightmare came. She'd been free of it for more than a year, although it had haunted her for months after Bryn died. Once again she was running along a Welsh riverbank, her screams alerting his kayak team. The river was turbulent that day, after a week of heavy rain. It would be fun, Bryn had said; why didn't Cass come and watch? She could get the barbecue started for when they'd finished. Then Greg, at nineteen the youngest and newest member of the group, started playing the fool. Bryn, after a previous trip, had warned him, without success. Soon the youth was in trouble. Bryn had deliberately stayed close, and so, altering course, came to help.

From her vantage point, Cass could see the tragedy unravel like a length of film. By the time she'd scrambled down the bank and raised the alarm, it was too late. Bryn had freed Greg from his kayak, but now Bryn's own craft was upturned beside it. Feverishly Greg was tearing at the deadly green ropes of weed that had trapped his rescuer. Cass plunged into the water, gasping as it threatened to drag her downstream. Grabbing a branch that overhung the bank, she fought alongside Greg.

At last there came the wail of sirens from the ambulance and police cars. Bryn was eventually cut free from a tangle of unseen tree roots, as strong as steel hawsers, which had twined themselves around his limbs. On her knees, as close as she could, Cass had watched the paramedics battle to save him. Eventually they lifted his still body into the ambulance.

Although the sirens were silent now, her ears rang with their sound. She awoke with a start, saturated with sweat, and shaking. There could be no more sleep. If she stayed in bed, the nightmare might come again.

She spent the rest of the day wrapped up on the couch, in front of the television. Each programme passed in a haze of movement and talk, but she saw and heard none of them.

Am I some sort of Jonah? Does my touch bring bad luck to the people I love?

She couldn't stop dreading the reason for Matt's long silence. In her mind she replayed every word of her conversations with Graham Stanthorpe. Everything that frightened her about a man who lived with adventure was coming true — for the second time! And this time she doubted her ability to drag herself out of the abyss. At last the tears came, heavy, deep-rooted, wracking her in a storm of weeping.

At midnight, still reluctant to go to bed, she stayed watching an old, not particularly enjoyable film, until her eyelids were drooping. But when she finally slept, it was a rainbow-coloured dream which entered her vision, not a nightmare. Bryn was there again, but this time he was laughing. He'd been windsurfing and was striding from the seashore in his wetsuit, sandy hair plastered to his skull, his big square teeth white against tanned cheeks. He was always smiling, relishing the challenges that nature presented, whether by sea, river or mountain. As Cass awoke, she was smiling too. He'd been happy, he'd lived his life to the full, and it was these memories that had penetrated her sleep.

This was what she wanted for Matt. She wanted him, too, to follow his dream and be fulfilled and happy, whatever the outcome. In the meantime, she mustn't sit around waiting like some pathetic hanger-on. Throwing aside the bedcovers, she went into the bathroom and turned on the shower. As the warm water sprayed her head and body, she lifted pale lips in a smile that begged the heavens for courage. Even now, perhaps the naval vessel that hovered close to the *Venus* might have negotiated its release and scared off the attackers. Or something.

A shudder went through her limbs; but then, stepping out of the shower and dragging a towel around herself, she straightened her shoulders. Matt would be back. Until he came, she had friends, family, and a job she loved. A small voice whispered that only when he was home again would she be truly complete. If the thought came that she was planning to fight the dragon of fear

221

with a pencil-sharpener, she pushed it away.

Next morning Cass decided she ought to stay at home for one more day. Her cough had worsened until her chest felt as though it had been sandpapered. No one would thank her for passing on a bug like this! She spent the morning indoors, after telephoning Lyn. Her friend was sympathetic and said the rest of the staff would be grateful if Cass would keep her germs to herself.

'Got everything you need?' the head teacher asked in her usual brisk fashion.

'I've swallowed a litre of cough mixture and I've got food in the cupboard, thanks. I'll see you at the coalface tomorrow!' Her cold was running its usual course, but with the help of pills, potions and paper tissues it should be on its way out by the morning.

Last night's dream had brought comfort and optimism. The alarm she'd felt when Anna first voiced anxiety about Matt hadn't exactly vanished, but she wasn't frightened anymore. There was still no word from him or from his head-quarters, but Cass told herself that no news was good news. If she wanted to marry Matt, this was a situation she'd got to expect. Of course she was uneasy! She longed to be sure that he was safe. But shipwreck and piracy were neurotic fantasies. It was true, they did happen in real life, but it would be crazy to imagine him drowned or kidnapped every time he didn't ring.

At lunchtime she made a mug of instant soup. It was hard to be interested in which packet to open; a cold took the flavour from everything. Still, something hot might ease her throat. The next stage was sure to be a silly tickle which could start a paroxysm of coughing as soon as she spoke. The other person would see that you couldn't talk, but invariably ask, 'Are you all right?' Amused at the idiocy of her thoughts, Cass wondered if she fancied minestrone or mushroom soup. Tomato didn't match her mood, but leek and potato might do.

She lifted the kettle, engrossed in

decision-making. Her hand jerked and boiling water shot across her wrist. Clutching her arm, she cried out in pain. It was the final, miserable moment after days of despair. Wretchedly, she wondered what else could go wrong. And then, despite all her good resolutions, the tears came again. Where, oh where was Matt?

The doorbell rang. Why now, for goodness' sake? It rang again. Could she pretend to be out? Most likely it was the postman with a package too large for the letterbox. Or it might be someone canvassing for local elections. There was no need to answer.

The bell was persistent this time, as though someone was leaning on the buzzer. Cursing under her breath, Cass went to open the door. Whoever it was, she could blame her red eyes and thickened voice on her cold.

Matt was there. The sight of him shattered her defences.

Throwing herself into his arms, she cried as though her heart was breaking.

She couldn't stop. Sobs wracked her body as she clung to him.

'Darling, you must stop this! You'll make yourself ill!' Kicking the door shut with his foot, Matt swung her up in his arms and carried her into the living room. Cass still wouldn't let go, her fingers clenched on his suede jacket. Tears coursed down her cheeks, wetting his shirt as she burrowed her face into his chest.

She hadn't cried like this since that long-ago day when her mother had died. It was as though even that, and the crying she'd done for Bryn, hadn't been enough. For days now she'd tried not to worry about Matt or to tell anyone about the danger surrounding the *Venus*. She'd spent a lonely weekend with her worst cold in years, and now she'd scalded herself and it hurt. Cass couldn't take any more.

Matt knew it. His eyes were unreadable as he sat on the couch, cradling her on his lap, stroking her hair with fingers that were unsteady.

Eventually the storm subsided until she rested, exhausted, against him. 'I'm sorry,' she whispered. 'I'm not usually such a weakling.'

'I am the one who should be sorry!' Matt closed his eyes, deep lines engraving his lean cheeks.

'I must look terrible!' Cass drew away slightly. 'I'll go and clean myself up.'

'You look wonderful'. Knowing she would recognise it as an outrageous lie, his mouth quirked, but his face was dark.

As Cass stood, she accidentally knocked her hand. Wincing, she held it against her breast.

Matt jumped up. 'What have you done?' Carefully he turned her wrist. The patch was angry, red and throbbing. 'What's this? What have you done to yourself?' he asked again.

She tried to pull away, but he wouldn't let go.

'It's nothing. A silly moment with the kettle. I'd only just done it — that's why you walked into a Cassandra Sutherland waterfall. It was the final straw after being run off my feet at work, and then stuck at home with the worst cold in history!' She managed a light tone and a watery smile. 'It really stung!' He mustn't suspect that it was the sight of him, safe and well, that triggered her breakdown.

Matt's expression was bleak as he examined her wrist. He made her hold it under the cold water tap for a while. She found a bandage, which he tied with care. His eyes were inscrutable, his mouth a straight line, even when he'd raided her refrigerator, saying they both needed to eat. In the kitchen he cooked omelettes, which they ate with salad and granary bread rolls, quickly defrosted when Cass took them from her freezer. It was the middle of the day, but he opened a bottle of wine and poured them each a glass, raising his in a toast without speaking.

'And now I want to know why the long silence,' she said when they had finished their meal. By unspoken agreement they'd talked only about her school activities until they were sitting on the couch, with a tray of coffee in front of them. 'There were two options. Either you'd found yourself another girlfriend, or you'd got wedding nerves and emigrated.'

'Neither.' His face was serious, and she knew that it was going to take time to reassure him that she hadn't been unduly worried. 'I hear that you've been to see Graham Stanthorpe. He wondered if he'd upset you with talk of pirates and so on.'

'Pirates?' said Cass vaguely. 'Oh yes, he did mention the possibility, except that you weren't in waters where they usually operate.'

'So you weren't too anxious?'

'Well, I must be honest.' Spreading her hands, she tried to keep a reasonably cheerful expression on a face that she suspected was still red and blotchy. 'I was ... just a bit. Then after talking to Mr. Stanthorpe, I realised the most likely problem was satellite failure.' She lifted the percolator. 'More coffee?'

'No. I mean ... no, thank you.' He looked at Cass thoughtfully. 'I must admit that I was worried about your reaction, and not without reason.'

'You mean Bryn.' It was best to be straightforward. This was no time to pretend.

'Yes. The *Venus* ran into a tropical storm, a particularly violent one that threw us off course. From then on we had radar and satellite problems too. And engine failure.'

Matt leant back against the cushions with a sigh. He looked tired, and she knew that in part, the blame was hers. After what must have been a gruelling voyage and then hours in a plane, the last thing he'd needed was a wet, disintegrating woman clinging to him.

'When we docked in Mombasa, I rang you but there was no answer. It seemed best to get the earliest flight to England, and I grabbed one that was almost ready to take off.' She realised that the telephone had interrupted her sleep, and not the siren heralding police and ambulance as they rushed to the Welsh river of her nightmare.

Matt yawned. It was easy to see that he was exhausted. When she pressed him to go, he admitted that he was looking forward to a shower and a long sleep. He made no mention of what had happened to the *Venus* after the storm except to say, 'There's a lot more to tell you. But it can wait till tomorrow.' Grinning crookedly, he kissed her eyes, her nose, her mouth and, dropping his arms, began to rise from the couch.

'Darling, I've got to sort out some data from my flat and fax it through to headquarters. Then I'm planning to fall into bed.' Standing, he quirked a dark eyebrow as he looked down at her. 'I wish it was your bed, my lovely, but I need clean clothes and a long sleep before I'm any use to man, woman or beast!'

'I hope I fall into the middle category!' Reaching up, she hugged him and pushed him gently towards the door.

14

After he'd gone, Cass told herself that she'd had a lucky escape. Matt seemed to accept that her only reaction to his long silence had been reasonable concern, and that the pain of scalding her wrist had caused the flood of tears, compounded by the shock of finding him at her door.

Admittedly, she had been close to panic after Anna's initial alert, and again when she spoke to Graham Stanthorpe in his office. And then had come his telephone call and the terrible news that the *Venus* had been captured. The days had been grey, edging towards black. How she'd resisted the temptation to confide in her father, Liz, or anyone else, she would never know.

Out of that discipline had come some sort of composure. She'd forced herself to assess the situation logically, and above all, keep calm. The corners of her mouth lifted, turning into a touch of triumph. This had been a trial run when it came to the worry stakes. She'd coped with it, and she'd do even better next time!

It was hard to stop smiling when she reached school the next day. Lyn took one look at her and said, 'No need to tell me! Matt's safe and well — hurray!' Giving Cass a hug, she advised, 'Take a lesson from this, old girl. Next time he hits a storm, just send him an umbrella.' As they laughed, Cass thanked the heavens that Lyn knew nothing of the *Venus* and the pirate attack. Her friend might have found that more difficult to brush aside!

As for Cass herself, she still didn't know the end of the story and how the survey team and ship's crew had reached safety. If Matt didn't willingly disclose what had happened once they'd been boarded by pirates, she was determined to tackle him, but suspected that he'd heavily edit whatever version he chose to present. She had realised that her fiancé was an intensely private man. In fact, there was little she knew about his earlier life, and somehow the chance to ask about it had never arisen.

On one occasion that first summer, sharing a jug of iced lemonade with Anna in her sunny courtyard whilst Matt served a customer, the Hungarian woman had mentioned his mother. When Cass asked more about her, Anna hesitated before saying, 'She did not care for travel, so Matthias only saw her when he came home from boarding school. But he often spent those holidays with his paternal grandparents.' At that point Matt had come to join them, having successfully sold a canvas. Anna changed the subject by teasingly offering congratulations on his salesman technique. Cass recognised she was being tacitly warned to say no more.

The day after Matt's return to England, Cass had scarcely reached home from a busy day when her doorbell rang again. She almost ran to open it this time. Yesterday already seemed a long time ago.

A newly invigorated Matt swept her into his arms, and then, taking her face between gentle hands, kissed her so thoroughly that she lost herself in the sheer sensation of feeling his mouth moving against hers, his breath on her cheeks, and the whipcord strength of his strong body drawing ever closer to hers. When he released her, they moved into her sitting room, where he wandered around, looking at the shelves filled with books, and framed pictures on the softly tinted walls, as though reassuring himself that he was once more in familiar territory.

Cass wasn't to know that this was what he needed. A lone wolf for so long, dedicated to his career, travelling and spending months away from various flats that he'd occupied, it felt unbelievably good to have someone to come back to, someone who gave the word 'home' real meaning at last. Unlike most people, 'home' wasn't something that he associated with precious childhood memories. With an effort, he shrugged the thought aside.

Before leaving Mombasa, he'd visited the hospital where Dave the apprentice, having been injured on board the *Venus,* was recovering from concussion. Once fit enough to travel, he'd return to England, hopefully within a few days. In the meantime, Matt's own flight didn't leave until evening, so there was time to stroll through the old town, away from wide, traffic-heavy thoroughfares and smart shops. He'd always liked these narrow streets, fringed on each side by a jumble of dilapidated stone buildings, and was amused to see the same graffiti he'd seen here before on many of the walls. It wasn't offensive, most singing the praises of Liverpool football team even here, scrawled by their African fans. The rough scrawls led on to other thoughts. If he and Cass had a son, would Matt become one of the fathers standing on the touchline? And what would be their daughter's interests? Would she be a miniature version of her mother, with fine fair hair and calm grey eyes? He hoped so.

Now, within reach of Cass, watching her move around the kitchen, he hoped so even more.

Guessing that Matt might be glad of a

change from ship and restaurant food, she had prepared a cheese fondue with crusty bread, one of his favourite meals, fun to eat and just right for special occasions. Opening a bottle of white wine, she told him lightly, 'We don't get anything like this with school dinners — just water — so I'm celebrating the end of my cold. And, I suppose, having my fiancé back in one piece, with no sign of storm damage!'

It wasn't until they had cleared the table and were seated comfortably that Cass finally acknowledged he didn't plan to say a word about the *Venus* and its adventures after being hit and blown off course by the storm. All he'd done while they ate was touch briefly on delays inevitably caused by the tropical weather. Casually he admitted the main frustration had come through lack of communication with the outside world. Most of the survey team and ship's crew were men who knew that lack of news or contact was one of the major worries for families waiting at home. They didn't like the fact but had to accept that it was part of the job.

Drawing a deep breath, Cass knew she must tackle him. Matt had got to realise that shielding her from the dangers he might encounter was no way to build an open, honest marriage. 'So now you're going to tell me about the pirate hijacking, aren't you?'

For an instant he said nothing. His long frame tensed in the armchair. Tightening muscles made his face the mask of a stranger. For a split second Cass wondered at the depths of emotion she'd unwittingly unleashed.

'Graham Stanthorpe!' Jerking upright, he issued a stream of words in his own tongue. She didn't understand them, but it didn't take much to guess.

He took no notice as she shot from her seat, grabbing his coffee before it went flying. So this was why Cass was close to hysteria when he arrived! Nothing to do with her being ill. Nothing to do with a scalded arm. Instead she'd lived an agony of fear, sharing his danger every step of the way.

'Darling, calm down!' Cass had jumped

237

up, her arms sliding around Matt's waist and for the first time receiving no response. She had a feeling he'd like to grab hold of Stanthorpe and shake the man till he begged for mercy. 'Mr. Stanthorpe isn't to blame! I pestered till he was forced to tell me what was happening!' Leaning back, she looked up into Matt's face, dark but with a whiteness around his mouth that told of controlled anger. 'Don't you see, I had to know the truth! It was no use him fobbing me off with tales of satellite failure and all that stuff. If I'm old enough to be your wife, then I'm old enough to be told if you're in danger. There's such a thing as prayer, you know, and even my tiny voice just might be heard!'

'Your tiny voice certainly was heard!' At last the hard lines began to smooth from his face, and pulling her down beside him on the couch, he wrapped his arms so tightly around Cass that although she was happy to be there, eventually she had to break free.

'That's enough, big guy! Let me

breathe!' Struggling upright, she tucked herself more comfortably into the curve of his shoulder and said, 'Tell me what happened. I want to know. I need to know.'

Releasing a long sigh, Matt began to talk. 'You obviously were told, or guessed, everything that happened when the storm caught us. We were swept off course, equipment damaged, engine fouled up, and communication lost.'

'Yes, I know all that. Now go on to the bits I don't know.'

'Stanthorpe, the fool, told you we'd been hijacked.' Fleetingly, he frowned. 'We knew there might be trouble once Evans — you will remember he is the captain — saw what we eventually recognised as the pirates' mother ship not far off. He put an extra watch on deck, but darkness and a quiet night, followed by heavy morning mist, hid the skiff they sent to board us.' A deep grunt gave some indication of his reaction. 'You have to congratulate these fellows — before we knew it, they'd flung up a ladder and grappling iron. One came up the ladder, and another up the rope, armed to the teeth. We'd been ordered not to resist, and in any case, two more were covering us from below.'

He didn't tell her how, whilst the pirates confronted the captain, Dave, the young survey apprentice, had lunged forward, only to be brutally hit with a rifle butt. He'd collapsed on the deck, blood pouring from his head. A crewman bent to help him, and he, too, was assaulted, falling beside Dave.

From Matt's momentary silence, Cass knew there was more, and that his recollection of something that had happened at that point was bleak. She knew better than to interrupt, but read a great deal into his deepened tone as he went on speaking.

'The pirate leader was a hard-eyed Arab, one who'd obviously done this before. What ruined his plan was that with engine failure, the *Venus* was useless to him and his masters who, presumably, were instructing the mother vessel from

240

some safe vantage point on land.'

Matt looked down at the total concentration on Cass's upturned face and smiled slightly as he brushed his lips across her smooth cheek.

'There were four pirates. The head man sent a couple down to the engine room. When they returned to the main deck, the older of the two said there was a problem — the *Venus* couldn't move. I can't speak their language, so I don't know the words the leader directed at his gods, but I doubt they were complimentary!' He caught Cass's fingers and kissed them as she pushed back the lock of his dark hair which, as always, refused to stay in place.

'You know there's quite a large international fleet patrolling those waters in recent years. In the beginning the attacks came from vigilante groups — fishermen protecting their waters. But today's piracy is highly organised and very profitable. The navy are only allowed to intervene when they catch vessels in the actual act, but are a useful deterrent. No pirate ship wants to fall foul of a fully armed frigate, so the essential strategy is to give attackers no opportunity to take hostages.'

'And that's what you did?'

'That's what the navy did!' At last Matt relaxed, shifting lower in his seat, though his arm remained as closely as ever around Cass. 'They sent up helicopters, one towards the mother ship, one coming close enough to the *Venus* to capture the Somalis' attention.'

'But didn't the pirates grab the captain, or someone, to make it clear they'd take hostages?'

'Yes.' Matt nodded. 'But then they stood watching as the first helicopter approached the mother vessel. Their ship fired its engines and moved off, leaving the four men from the skiff stranded. At that point our 'visitors' must have been concerned, to put it mildly.' Briefly he paused, wry amusement lifting his lips. 'They could capture hostages by the dozen, but with no functioning vessel to take them home, they would be reliant on a hostile military vessel that was bristling with men and firepower.'

'So what happened next?'

'Well, next they started shooting at the second helicopter that left the frigate. It came near enough to attract their attention but kept moving, and did its best to stay out of range. At the same time, of course, the attackers were holding Evans. They didn't realise that on the port side behind them, the *Venus* had been quietly boarded by naval frogmen.' Again, his mouth tilted. 'The Somalis didn't know what hit them!'

'How did you get back to port? Did the frigate tow you?'

This time Matt laughed out loud, his teeth gleaming white in the dim glow from the softly lamp-lit room. 'No. When the raiders were taken aboard the navy vessel, Sparks came up from the engine room. Evans asked if there was any chance of repairing the engines, or if we must ask for help. Sparks pulled both hands from his overall pockets with the widest grin we had seen in days. 'No, sir,' he said. 'It just so happens I've got the crucial bits here. Forgot about them

all the time we'd got visitors!' Evans
clapped him on the back and joined in
the laughter.'

15

During the next two weeks, despite the completion of reports and statistics for the education authorities and general end-of-year chaos at school, Cass and Matt managed to spend hours together when she wasn't working. Matt had to travel to his headquarters in central London each morning, but the evenings were largely free. Their new apartment was in a good state of repair, but Matt said that he would enjoy redecorating some of the rooms with shades of paint they both preferred. He would move in shortly, but Cass wouldn't give up her own flat until they married.

'Pastel emulsion is a long cry from your usual style!' Cass had come directly from work. They'd agreed to eat later at an inexpensive bistro that was only five minutes away. Walking into the main bedroom, where he'd transformed the colour scheme, she joked that she would miss the ivy-twined wallpaper chosen by the previous occupier.

'Would you like a mural?' Matt quirked a dark eyebrow. 'Perhaps a field of sunflowers on the wall facing our bed?'

Vigorously, Cass shook her head. 'No. I might spend too much time admiring them, and neglect my husband.'

'In that case, I shall paint it an insipid grey.' His arms were tightly around Cass as he rubbed his cheek against her hair. She breathed in the familiar scent of aftershave, the heat of his body, and the tang of paint, with a sigh of contentment. Every day she was learning more about Matt, his dry sense of humour, his intelligence and humanity. Under a quiet exterior she'd found a man of principle, but one who was flexible and ready to hear other points of view. Lyn had called him 'Mr. Nice Guy' after they'd met, and so he was.

There was just one thing that Cass wondered about. When she asked Matt if he ever lost his temper, he grinned and told her to wait and see. She'd seen how he reacted to injustice or cruelty, and didn't doubt that on some occasions he felt the intense anger he'd directed at Stanthorpe, blaming the man for telling Cass so much and causing additional fear. At other times, he would throw his newspaper down in disgust and give a colourful description of a particular article or journalist. Although they rarely watched television, Cass found secret enjoyment in his scathing asides, especially when it came to politics or climate change.

'Would you like me to turn the sound off?' she'd teased one evening at her flat. 'I'm sure your commentary would be more interesting!'

Matt made a face at her and promised to keep quiet. 'But only if I can punch your cushions instead!'

Perhaps he'd been rightly furious about Stanthorpe scaring her, but Cass found herself waiting for Matt to lose his calm about the everyday things of life. Did she really know any of the deeper emotions that drove this man who held her heart?

He'd been irritated when she dipped a cream-coated brush into a white tin of paint, and exasperated when she leant against a still-wet door-jamb. Even so, it wasn't what Cass regarded as losing his cool. Normally slow to anger, her own composure could explode into fiery fragments when something or someone pushed her too far, though the moment passed quickly and she never sulked. She warned Matt that when the moment came, he'd need to run for cover.

At the beginning of the third week, he moved into their new home, bringing those items of his furniture which they both wanted to keep. They'd been lucky to find such a lovely flat within reasonable distance of both the school and Matt's headquarters. A one-time lodge, the stately home it once guarded had been swallowed by a housing estate. Fortunately, the building still retained the privacy afforded by a surround of trees and evergreen shrubs.

Inside their private entrance, the hall led to a pleasant sitting room, large enough to comfortably accept newly built bookshelves, Matt's sofa and armchairs, and the rosewood table that had belonged to Cass's grandmother. Glass doors opened onto a lawn with views across the adjoining park. The open-plan kitchen had plenty of room for table and chairs, so if they had dinner guests, 'She who cooks won't be stuck out of sight and hearing in another room,' Cass had commented, with a sidelong glance at Matt, who had raised his black eyebrows and said, 'She?'

From the hallway, a passage led not only to two fair-sized bedrooms, but also a smaller room designated as Matt's study. There was even a cubbyhole that, once furnished, would give shelter to Cass and her own paperwork.

Each apartment possessed its own front door, and the other residents, two older couples, appeared pleasant but not intrusive. When Matt was away, Cass thought, it would be nice to know she wasn't entirely alone. There wouldn't be the same camaraderie she'd enjoyed with

Magda, but life had changed — grown better — for both of them.

Cass, like Matt, had been packing her belongings. She couldn't wait to join him. Her flat had been a convenient base for several years, but it breathed a mixture of good and less good memories. The landscape she'd purchased from Matt in Szentendre had not been harmed by its spell of solitary confinement in the back of her cupboard. It held new significance now, and she loved the painting because it marked their first meeting. Who could have dreamed that one day she and the tall, dark Hungarian with clear grey-blue eyes would be hanging it together? This weekend she planned to leave here, and would stay with her father and Liz until the wedding.

Arriving at the new flat late one afternoon, she decided to make a start on the small room which Matt would use as a study. They'd already chosen the paint, a pale oyster grey, with white woodwork, but the window frames needed rubbing down and undercoating before they were given a finishing coat of gloss paint.

The telephone shrilled soon after she started work. Dropping the sandpaper, she lifted the receiver. The caller was Matt's friend, Paul.

'Hi there! You must be Cass! I know we'll meet at the wedding, but Fran and I wondered if you and Matt could manage dinner with us tomorrow night. Sorry it's short notice, but we're not as organised as we might be. Our lives are dominated by a three-year-old and his crowded diary.'

Cass knew that Paul was home again, having finished the first stage of his project off the Australian coast, and that his wife Frances, or Fran, worked part-time as a teaching assistant. School terms coincided nicely with Tim's playgroup hours, but Matt had chuckled as he described Fran's attempts at housekeeping. 'Paul always describes them as 'interesting', but I think there are times when he needs that famous sense of humour that we all rely on.'

As Cass replaced the receiver, she was smiling. Paul sounded just like she'd imagined, and she felt that Fran might prove a kindred spirit when it came to her own housekeeping efforts. Living alone, it hadn't mattered if the washing-up wasn't always done, or if last night's jumper was slung on the back of the chair, or if sunshine betrayed the lack of a duster. She wouldn't class herself as anything but normal, and it was a comfort having a stepmother like Liz who freely raised her hand and confessed to being the same.

It hadn't occurred to Cass that Matt might not be keen to accept Paul's invitation. 'I more or less said yes, thanks very much, we'd love to come!' she said, dismayed by his lukewarm reception.

'Well, it sounds as though we're committed.' He sounded unusually grumpy but caught her look of surprise. 'Sorry, darling! It's just that sometimes I tire of talking about work — and that's what happens when Paul and I are together, especially as we haven't met for several months.'

For much of the following evening, however, the men avoided talking about oceans and what lay beneath them. Paul and Fran lived in a small detached house near Hampstead Heath which, they said, was an ideal location now they had Tim.

'It gives him freedom to run around with other children, and I love wandering across the heath,' said Fran. 'I was so excited when I first saw the house where Keats wrote 'Ode to a Nightingale' — he was always my favourite poet. I'm glad we didn't study him in any depth at school, because that's a sure way to murder any piece of literature!'

Although Cass was half-inclined to agree, Matt and Paul thought otherwise, so discussion across the dinner table was lively, interrupted only when Tim wandered downstairs asking for a drink. Dark-haired like his mother, and with the same elfin features and quicksilver movements, Cass didn't find it hard to believe Fran when she said that keeping house was fun, so long as you made life interesting by putting things like shirts and pants away in the wrong place. 'It keeps Paul on his toes,' she said jauntily.

'And how! Especially when I turn up at headquarters wearing odd socks,' her husband complained, grinning all the same.

They were a well-matched couple, thought Cass. She had liked Paul immediately. Fairly short and stocky, with a thatch of straight fair hair, he had bright blue eyes that he said came from Swedish forbears. His appearance and personality formed a complete contrast to his lively wife, although her engaging warmth made Cass feel, as the evening progressed, that she could ask how Fran had coped when Paul came close to death, his diving gear sabotaged. After dinner the men had gone into the small room where Paul kept his work materials, describing it as 'refuge from the chaos' that occasionally erupted in other areas of the house.

'It was awful,' admitted his wife frankly. 'I was horrified, terrified ... Every emotion you could name, I went through it.'

'Did you know about Paul's work — that it took him into dangerous waters sometimes — before you married?' Cass asked.

Fran looked surprised. 'Of course! I got him to tell me all about ocean currents, the seabed, weather hazards. He taught me to dive, and I made sure he took me underwater into some fairly scary places. I wanted to know everything, despite dreading possible trouble one day. But who could dream it would come in the shape of a murderous thug named Hans?' Her eyes flashed, and it was easy to see that Hans would do well to stay hidden. 'We'd all assumed he was a decent guy, just filling in while Matt was ill.'

'But Tim had been born by then. You had to face bringing him up alone, fatherless.' Cass looked into Fran's face, noticing for the first time the fine lines that fanned out from her hazel eyes and the way her mouth compressed as she remembered the weeks when Paul had been kept in a medically induced coma. 'When it was over and Paul had recovered, surely you talked about him moving to some other job?'

Vigorously, Fran shook her head.

'Not on your life!' The glance she shot at Cass was compassionate and held understanding. 'Paul loves what he does. Why should I want to change him? This is the man I fell in love with.' Suddenly lightening the mood, she giggled, back to the everyday Fran. 'After all, what's the point of knitting a purple jumper and immediately dying it green?'

Cass laughed at the analogy, knowing what she meant, but her mood was reflective as they made coffee and took it to the sitting room, where Matt and Paul soon joined them.

16

Five days before the wedding ceremony, Liz held a dinner party. 'There's never enough time to talk to anyone on the day,' she announced. 'So I thought it would be nice for us to meet and spend some quality time together first.'

'Quality time!' Peter looked amused. 'Who will be your victims?'

Lifting her chin in disdain, she listed Anna, Istvan and Lili, who, with Rudi, the baby, were spending the week with friends in London. Magda and Zoltan had also accepted her invitation. Regular family members Reg, Molly and David would be present, and two of Peter's cousins.

Paul was to be best man at the wedding. When Liz asked Matt if his friend and Fran would be free to join them for dinner, Matt hesitated for a moment before thanking her and said that they'd almost certainly like to come but had occasional baby-sitting problems. He promised to telephone Paul later. Cass, sensitive to her fiancé's reactions, had a feeling that he wasn't enthusiastic about them joining the group, and it puzzled her.

She was glad when Fran telephoned to say that she and Paul would love to be there, and that a neighbour whose son was the same age as Tim had offered to look after him for the night. 'Tim'll be in his seventh heaven,' she said. 'I don't know what time they'll get to sleep, but he can catch up the next day. I hope his mood isn't too grotty!'

Most of the other guests had arrived before Paul and Fran rang the doorbell, and soon Liz's spacious sitting room was filled with easy conversation and laughter. Matt was fully occupied as one of the hosts, but every so often Cass would feel his eyes upon her, their expression making any other communication un-necessary. Later, she knew, he would find some way of stealing a short while when they could be alone.

As Liz circulated with a tray of drinks,

two of her workmates emerged from the kitchen carrying trays of hors d'oeuvres. It was easy to see that they, too, worked in the fashion trade, both clad in simple but stylish summer evening wear. David, Liz's brother, moved closer. His pleasant face brightened. With the expertise of a man who appreciated female company, he was quick to start chatting to the youngest, a shapely redhead. It seemed that he had completely forgotten Monique, the chef at the restaurant in France! Liz whispered that she'd spent such a fortune on the pre-dinner nibbles that only the most elegant 'waitresses' would do them justice.

Slipping a tiny vol-au-vent in her mouth with a sigh of ecstasy, Cass looked around to make sure that everyone was happy, helped herself to a glass of sparkling wine, and went to say hello to Paul. He greeted her with a warm smile, and after hearing about Tim's latest prank, she led him to a corner away from the noisier part of the room.

'Everything ready for the big day?' he asked.

'Just about,' said Cass, 'although it's a pity that Matt's mother can't be at the wedding. But it is a long journey from the Caribbean, of course. Have you ever met her?'

Paul looked across to where Matt and Peter were deep in conversation with David. 'Only once,' he said. 'And that was briefly.'

'She'll soon be my mother-in-law, so I'm curious to know what she's like.'

'Ghastly!' Fran suddenly materialised beside her. 'Utterly self-centred and ultra-feminine in the worst sense of the word!'

'Fran!' Paul shot her a warning glance, and then in a long-suffering tone told Cass, 'Don't take any notice of my wife. She's exaggerating the few comments I made. In any case, I only met her for a couple of hours when Matt and I were on a stopover that happened to be in Bermuda, where she lives.'

Fran drifted away with an unrepentant grin, but Cass knew this was perhaps her only chance to find more about the forces that had shaped Matt into the man she knew. 'Paul, you know how reticent Matt is about his childhood,' she said. 'I don't ever want to hurt him by saying the wrong thing, so please can you tell me just a little more? I know his father was an architect who died when Matt graduated, and that his mother remarried. But that's all.'

Rubbing a hand across his eyes, Paul's reluctance was painfully evident, but after a moment he relented. 'His father was a top-notch architect, in fact, so his work often took him abroad. Matt's mother could have gone as well more often than not, but she didn't care for travel. On the other hand, she didn't like staying at home without him. It didn't make for a happy marriage. Matt has never said much, but I gather he grew up in an atmosphere of constant rows, and was relieved when they shipped him off to boarding school.'

Looking across the room and seeing Matt still deep in conversation, he went on, 'A few years after his parents divorced, Matt's father died, and his mother soon married a wealthy man quite a few years older than herself. He cossets and pampers her, and she revels in the attention.' Ruefully he added, 'Not my sort of woman.'

'And not Matt's.' Touching Paul's arm briefly, Cass said, 'Thank you. I'm truly grateful.'

Paul changed the subject, asking her opinion on recent education reforms. As he said, in no time at all Tim would be moving on to primary education, but nursery school had given him a good start.

Before long, Liz, elegant as ever in a copper-gold sheath dress, entered the room and called, 'Dinner is served. Come and get it!'

The meal was delicious, and Liz was obviously gratified to see her guests eat with flattering enthusiasm. The first course, served in shell-shaped glass dishes, was a small cluster of walnut pieces in a tangy dressing, nestling in a crisp bed of rocket leaves. For anyone who preferred it, there were melon balls and slivers of Parma ham. After that came succulent chicken breast with mangetout, baby potatoes and a wonderful sauce, followed by a selection of desserts. Liz's two glamorous friends helped clear away each course, and coffee was served quite soon after they all moved into the sitting room.

Soon Cass found herself talking to Paul again. She liked him. He was easy company, and perhaps in some recess of her mind was the hope, and pleasure, of hearing anecdotes about the man she was engaged to, his likes and dislikes, and the unusual places and friends he and Paul had known. 'Will you be continuing your work in Australia?' she asked.

'No; I've completed my part of the job. I'm due for a short holiday, but then I'll be joining the *Venus* again next month and getting stuck into an entirely new survey.'

Cass already knew, having pressed Matt for the information, that the vessel had undergone repairs after its battering in the tropics. Despite that, as well as the pirate attack, the survey team had concluded its research, so there was no need to return to the same location in the Indian Ocean. It was hard for Cass to hide her relief.

'Matt will be glad to be working with you again,' she said, 'no matter where you're sent.'

Paul took a long swig of his drink. 'Yes.'

'I gather you don't know yet where the next contract will take you.'

'No, not yet.'

Fran was threading her way towards the water jug which stood on the sideboard alongside a selection of soft drinks and wine. Paul caught her arm, pretending to measure the liquid left in the bottom of her glass. With a mock sigh he said, 'Okay madame. If I have to carry you home, that's what husbands are for I suppose.'

'Stoopid! It's a lovely citrus lemon juice, and I'm going to ask Liz where she bought it.' As she lunged at him, he grinned and, pulling her close, dropped a loud, smacking kiss on the corner of her mouth. Fran didn't stay, but went to where Peter was opening the French windows and, with a small group, wandered onto the patio.

It was good to see Paul's lively wife enjoying herself; but apart from her saucy interruption earlier, she and Cass hadn't really spoken. On arrival, Fran had commented briefly on Tim's delight at spending the night with his friend; but although the other guests were strangers, she quickly introduced herself and moved away.

Running a hand through her hair, Cass worried her bottom lip slightly and wondered why she felt uneasy. When she first greeted the couple tonight, Fran had seemed quiet, even restrained. It certainly wasn't fear of meeting new people. That wasn't in her nature! Perhaps she and Paul had had an argument before they arrived. But no, they appeared completely relaxed in each other's company, so it couldn't be that. So what was the problem?

Liz's brother was making himself useful

by bringing ice cubes into the room. With a word of excuse to Cass, Paul moved away and helped him clear a space on the sideboard. They exchanged a few comments about their work and soon started talking about Sweden, where Reg had spent holidays in his youth. Fran was chatting to Peter Sutherland on the patio. It looked as though she was admiring the geraniums, his pride and joy.

Others began to drift further into the long garden, lovingly planted with summer borders and flowering shrubs which perfumed the night air. Cass went with them, content to be with friends and family, and to know that Matt was there. As the evening progressed, she noticed several empty glasses on the round table near the summerhouse and wandered over to collect them, her sandals noiseless on the grass.

'I shall miss you, but I understand.' It was Paul's voice. He was standing in the angle of the ivy-clad garden wall where a tall lime tree cast its shadow. As Cass reached to pick up a glass, the soft green folds of her skirt fluttered and caught his attention.

'Cass!' He broke off whatever he'd been about to say and came forward into the light of small lanterns which Peter had strung along the paths. 'You're doing the chores! I'll give you a hand.'

He'd been talking to Matt, Cass realised. She made some sort of flippant response as Matt came from the shade and, slipping his arm around her, dropped a kiss on the fair hair that flicked her ears. For the rest of the evening she circulated amongst the guests, and so did Matt. When he looked at her there was no need to speak. All the same, she felt a prickle of unease. Slowly it became more acute. His love was easy to read, but his more private thoughts were hidden behind an expression that was ... downright bland.

17

The next morning, Cass left her father's house as soon as she had helped clear away all traces of the dinner party. Matt had said he'd like to paint the entrance hall of their apartment today, so she guessed that was where she would find him. During the night she'd repeated the words Paul had spoken to Matt over and over again. Eventually she knew there could only be one explanation.

When she arrived, she peeped through the letterbox before inserting her key in the lock. It wouldn't do to knock the bridegroom off a ladder just before the wedding. Her involuntary smile faded as she contemplated the battle ahead.

Matt was in the kitchen, stirring a tin of paint. His face lit with pleasure as, without a word, he straightened and held out his arms. Walking directly into the warmth of his hold, Cass prayed that she would get it right. So much depended on the next half-hour.

Always sensitive to her mood, Matt held her away slightly so that he could look directly into her eyes. 'What's the problem, my love? Tell me. And then we'll have a coffee break.'

Cass sailed straight into combat. There was no point in wasting time. 'I overheard Paul last night. I didn't mean to eavesdrop. He said that he would miss you. Why?'

'Ah, yes.' He dropped his arms and frowned at the paint as though he wasn't entirely sure it was the right colour. His next words came carefully, as though he was placing a child's building blocks in exactly the right position. 'We don't always work together. I expect he told you about the project he has been concentrating on, north of Australia. Possibly he will return there, or move on to another part of the world. There is always need for geological surveys.'

'He told me his part of the Australian project's finished and he's returning to the *Venus* in a month's time,' Cass said innocently. 'Didn't you know?'

A grunt was the only indication that Matt heard her as he started removing the stick which he'd been using to stir the paint.

'We'll be home from our honeymoon by then,' she pointed out quietly. 'Surely you're not due for extra leave?'

Matt thrust the stick in a jar, jammed the lid onto the paint and, with a concentrated effort, opened a different tin. Cass counted several seconds as she waited for an answer.

'No. I shall be working in our London office for a while,' he said at last. His accent had deepened, a sign that she recognised. Matt was uneasy, and away from his comfort zone.

'For how long?' she persisted.

He shrugged. 'I am not certain.' Stretching past her to shift the stepladder to another position, he warned her not to brush against the wet woodwork. 'I've already had to redo the door frame that you wrecked the other day!'

The edge to his tone was so unlike anything she'd known from him that it confirmed her worst suspicions. 'You wouldn't have been crazy enough to opt for a laboratory job, would you? Or even a desk job?' She gripped the stepladder so that he couldn't take it away. 'And by that, I'm talking about a desk and a nice patterned carpet in your London headquarters!'

One look at his averted face told Cass she was right. Bending, with no chance to meet her eyes, he rummaged amongst the clutter of decorating materials. Her voice sharpened.

'Why? Why in heaven's name would you do that?'

He didn't answer immediately but ran a finger along his jaw, something she recognised as a give-away sign of discomfort. His attitude was so different from his usual composed manner that Cass knew she had him at a disadvantage. He hadn't yet prepared the words he would have used to tell her, whenever he judged the best time. She wondered how he would

271

have wrapped them up to make the change sound like a positive career move.

'It's because of me, isn't it?' she insisted. 'That's why you weren't keen for Paul to come to Liz's dinner last night. You were scared he'd let the cat out of the bag.'

'Don't be ridiculous.' Abruptly he straightened and faced her. A tinge of colour in his cheeks made his eyes more blue than grey, and his mouth was set in a way she hadn't previously known.

'Don't call me ridiculous!' As if he'd lit the touch-paper to a firework, the effect was the same. Her mood, increasingly explosive from the time she'd gone to bed last night until the moment she faced him this morning, was a volcano ready to erupt. 'If we want to describe each other, I'll soon find something for you! How about sneaky and secretive?'

Matt's head jerked back. He didn't like that at all! Well, she thought wrathfully, tough! 'Why didn't you tell me what you were planning?'

His brows drew together in a heavy frown. Beneath them, his eyes narrowed, but she could see them glitter. He couldn't have made it more obvious that he resented being questioned.

'There was no point in mentioning it until after the wedding,' he returned brusquely. 'By then, the arrangements will be finalised.'

'Then you'd better un-arrange them!' Cass tossed each word like a pebble on a tin tray. She couldn't believe that he'd made such a momentous decision without even hinting at what he had in mind. 'This is a major change. It'll affect both of us! The least you could do was talk about it — with me, the woman you're engaged to, not with your buddy, Paul!'

'I beg your pardon, Miss Sutherland! I'm sorry you are annoyed. I didn't realise that I must ask your permission.' His sarcasm made Cass blink. 'My new position will be more suitable for a married man.' He was imitating a concrete lamp-post, she decided. In fact, a block of cement would show more animation. It enraged her, as did his perception of her as some inadequate Victorian 'miss'.

'Well, as a married woman, it darned well won't suit me!' Her voice rose. 'You love working at sea. You've decided to give it up for my sake!' As he swung away, she blocked his path. 'I won't let you do it!'

'For goodness' sake!' At last, Matt erupted. 'What the hell do you want, woman?' He slammed his hand against the newly painted door. Cursing fluently, he snatched a rag and scrubbed at his fingers. 'You've talked yourself into accepting the fact that I enjoy what I do. But the truth is exactly the opposite. Admit you were near to collapse when I reached home!' Control fled as he towered over her like some dark avenger. 'Admit it!' he snapped.

'You've got it all wrong!' Shoving her hand a few inches from his face, Cass ticked off each finger one by one. 'First, I'd got a lousy cold and a graveyard cough.' Her blazing eyes dared him to interrupt. 'Second, I'd been stuck alone in a germ-ridden flat for three days. Third, you sat on my doorbell. Why you wouldn't clear off like any normal person when I didn't answer, I couldn't understand! As a result, I scalded myself. And it hurt like crazy. Of course I was in a state!'

'Don't pretend.' By now he was shouting too. 'You were sick with worry — and I was the cause!'

Desperately Cass tried to leash her temper. 'I was anxious that no one could contact your ship. But then I looked at the situation logically. I'd committed myself to sharing your life, whatever that entailed. When the *Venus* disappeared, I realised that was part of the package and I'd better get used to it.' She looked up at a grim-faced Matt. 'I can't let my world grind to a halt each time you leave home, whatever the reason for it!'

His face said he wasn't convinced. How could she make him believe her?

'When we first met, I was still terrified of losing people, whatever the reason,' she said. 'I'd allowed water to become a monster, out of all proportion to reality. But I've conquered that fear, whether you're on the sea or in the sea. My own life is important too. And I'm going to make the most of it.'

'You admit you were anxious. It was more than that.' He wasn't going to give way. Lips compressed, he stared at the floor. 'I should not have asked you to marry me, but for a while I was tempted. And then came the storm, the pirates and your tears. I knew it had to end.' Raising his head, he said, 'I could not risk losing you. There was no choice but to leave the seas.'

It was a sacrifice that Cass wasn't even tempted to accept. There could be no happiness for either of them unless they walked side by side into their marriage. As his hand came out to touch her arm, she slapped it away. From the look on his face, she'd landed him a whack on the jaw. A fresh spiral of flame was uncoiling inside her.

'I'll tell you this, Matthias Benedek! You don't know me at all! If you did, you'd never shape yourself into a different mould just to please me! It wasn't easy to explain how and why I'd changed. You pretended to believe me. But that was a lie! Underneath the pretence, you assume I've less courage than Anna or Fran, or all those other women who wait for their men.'

Why should she plead? Unconsciously he was equating her with his mother — by all accounts a weak-natured, selfish woman, ultra-feminine in a way which gave that sex a bad name. Firstly Anna had skirted the facts of Matt's upbringing, although his own reticence had revealed a vacuum there; and now, from Fran, Cass had learnt Paul's opinion of the woman he'd met at her home in Bermuda.

'I know your mother couldn't stand being alone when your father had to be away, but how dare you suggest that I'm the same?'

'Leave my parents out of it! You know nothing!' White-faced, his self-control fled; but before he could say any more, Cass, incandescent by now, hissed:

'Very well. Let's take it a step further. D'you realise that from the lofty heights where you've made this decision, you've

277

also barred me from having children?'

'What are you talking about?' As his fury matched her own, Cass felt a burst of satisfaction that at last she'd made him drop his mask. Their future together hung on the brink of a precipice as steep as any she'd yet encountered, but she dared not give way.

'As you've decided to protect me from all stress, anything to cause me concern, there's no chance you'd allow me to suffer childbirth! Have you considered that, you … you …' Words failed her and she stopped, breathless, but only for a moment. 'I thought you were an artist and marine geologist. I was wrong. You're an outdated Victorian dinosaur — one I don't want to know!'

As he opened his mouth to retaliate, she wrenched open the door and stormed out, slamming it behind her.

Matt caught her when she was half-way down the path. Incredibly, he was laughing. 'How dare you walk out when I'm talking to you!' He grabbed Cass and hauled her close. Holding her between paint-stained hands, he lifted her until her feet left the ground, and kissed her until she stopped struggling and her lips began to move against his.

'And how dare you leave me to finish the decorating alone? There won't be time after our honeymoon, because the *Venus* won't wait for the paint to dry!'

Cass's tears overflowed as she understood his meaning. 'So you'll go back to sea?'

His lopsided smile was back. 'Stop nagging me! I promise!'

18

The day of their wedding was sunny and filled with enchantment. The church was small, old, beautiful, and perfumed with the scent of flowers that Liz and her band of helpers had arranged the day before. The building was packed to capacity. As well as her father, stepmother and most of their relatives, Cass was delighted that Matt's Hungarian friends were here, people he regarded as family, as well as colleagues from his work. To her amusement, he'd even relented and invited Graham Stanthorpe, saying he understood how the man had crumbled when faced with a pint-sized firebrand who was more threatening than any tropical storm. Lyn and several teacher pals from school looked spectacular, having talked clothes and hats for weeks. Gathered beside them were friends Cass had known from childhood.

Her white satin gown fitted her slim frame perfectly. As she stood with Matt before the altar, a shaft of sunlight filtered through the stained-glass windows, touching with gold the simple lines of the dress and the tiny cream roses of her headdress.

When they left the building and stood on the cobblestoned path outside the porch, Matt lifted her hand and pressed his lips to the shining gold band on her finger. 'You look wonderful, Mrs. Benedek!'

'You look pretty good yourself, Mr. B!' Her smile was radiant as he stood beside her. 'Tall, dark and handsome. Just what I ordered!'

Matt's well-tailored dark grey suit and crisp white shirt could have made him seem an elegant stranger, but those luminous blue-grey eyes, high cheekbones and lopsided grin reassured her that this was Matt, and she knew he loved her.

One greeting card had touched Cass immensely, although her eyes misted as she read the enclosed letter. It came from Bryn's mother, Edna Weston. She wrote that she'd enjoyed sharing a home with her sister since leaving England but was beyond happy that soon she would be marrying Ken and moving into a new home which they'd bought together. She went on to say that although she would have loved Cass to be her daughter-in-law, she was genuinely delighted that Bryn's sweetheart had found love again. With fond memories in her heart, she was sending every good wish for a joyful marriage, and ended her letter by reminding Cass that she and Matt would be welcome visitors 'Soon, I hope'.

Matt's mother had also sent a card, a lavish one with a scrawled message saying that she was sorry her health prevented her from attending her only son's wedding, and that she couldn't wait to meet her new daughter-in-law. An open invitation to the couple to visit her and Duggie, her husband, accompanied a promise to give them a wonderful wedding present, but they must come to Bermuda and collect it. Matt passed the card to Cass without comment.

The reception continued into early evening, and so it wasn't until early the next morning that the newlyweds set off for Scotland, which Cass had never visited. Keen to spend as much time there as possible, they flew north before collecting the car which Matt had hired. Edinburgh featured high on Cass's list of places to visit, and she wasn't disappointed.

'What did you tell me at Visegrád?' Matt teased as she lingered over a bookshelf, torn between a huge selection of guidebooks.

'You mean that I'll have no time to read, learn and inwardly digest them all before we move on to the next 'site of great historic interest'?' Cass turned down the corners of her mouth in mock resignation and put one back on the shelf.

'Well, you must have bought at least a dozen by now!'

'But it's such a wonderful city, and there's so much I want to know about it.'

'We'll come again,' he promised. 'But tomorrow we should move on if you want to see more of Scotland.'

A few days later, after driving in a leisurely way through magnificent countryside, and lingering beside breath-taking lochs and harbours, they chose to take the ferry, rather than the modern bridge, to Skye.

'The Misty Isle,' breathed Cass as she saw the Cuillin Hills. Their slopes formed a strangely alien backdrop as they loomed low through the haze which hid them until early afternoon. 'They're so different, almost as though they belong on the moon.'

The crofter's snug cottage which they had rented was close to the water, and tucked into a crescent-shaped hollow. They had stocked up with food on leaving the ferry, and been assured that milk could always be had at the small shop half a mile distant.

It was a remote and beautiful hideaway, and Cass couldn't believe that she was here, alone with Matt, her husband, a fiery but tender lover. She knew that he'd had one or two casual romances in the past, but when she tried to ask more about them, Matt teased her for being inquisitive and said he'd only been practising because 'I knew a neat little history teacher would come along one day!'

'Why don't we hire bicycles?' Cass suggested on their second day. 'Then we can enjoy the scenery, smell the heather, and meet people more easily.'

Although the weather varied from day to day, it didn't keep them indoors. Matt carried sketchpad and pens in his saddle-bag, and Cass filled hers with picnic food and some of the guidebooks she was still accumulating. While Matt sat sketching, she caught up with the details of places they'd visited. Her love of history was fed by the ruined castles and crofts they saw as they explored the island. One morning they followed a rough path to a cave where Bonnie Prince Charlie hid after the Battle of Culloden.

'It's so romantic,' said Cass as they followed the cleft which led back into the cliff.

'It won't be romantic if we stay too long. The tide will turn again soon,' Matt warned. 'I've no desire to make love to you in wet socks.'

One evening, after they'd eaten in front of the fire, Matt took her right hand in his and looked closely at the ring she always wore. Silver, of Celtic design, it was charming.

'It belonged to my mother.' Cass touched the ring affectionately. 'I'm glad to bring it home again for a while. Dad bought it for her before I was born. They'd come to Skye for a late holiday, and she fell in love with both — the island, and the ring.' Memory was etched across her face, as well as a trace of sadness, as she said, 'I don't need the ring to remind me of her, but I love it just as she did.'

'I'm sorry you lost her, but she'll always be there — a loving, special part of you.'

He understood, and that sensitivity made Cass want so much to share, and try to ease, the pain of his own memories. Greatly daring, she whispered: 'I wish you could feel that same warmth for your own mother.'

Matt was quiet for a moment. Then he

spoke, almost as though he was dragging words from a dark, fathomless well. 'You already know that my parents' marriage was a miserable episode in our lives. My father was an architect when they met, but his career blossomed and soon he became one of his company's leading men. It meant that he often went abroad, either for brief assessment trips, or for longer spells once planning and construction began. My mother went with him at first, hated it, and eventually refused to go. By then, they had me.' He added wryly, 'I have no idea why. She has no interest in children and no motherly instinct whatsoever. It was a relief when they sent me to boarding school, away from the inevitable quarrels whenever he came home.'

'Did you like your school?' asked Cass quietly, knowing she must keep him talking.

'I made good friends, and spent my longer holidays with my father's family in Florida.' The strain left his face as briefly he grinned and tightened his arm around her. 'Good water sports!'

'I see where I must point the finger of blame.' She reached to place a butterfly kiss on his jaw.

'It was almost a relief when my parents divorced and within a couple of years my mother remarried. Her new husband was a wealthy retired man with a luxurious home in Bermuda.' Matt's tone had lightened as he added ruefully, 'It was the realisation of her wildest dreams!'

'But your father died?'

He nodded. 'Soon after I graduated. We met up a few times and liked each other, but I can't tell you that there was much, if any, love there either. He was a businessman, wedded to his work.'

'Still, you did inherit something special from him,' suggested Cass.

'What do you mean?' His eyebrows shot up, almost as though, she thought sadly, he couldn't believe anything good could remain of his childhood.

'Your talent as an artist, of course.'

Almost reluctantly, he nodded once more, and then his mouth quirked in the way she loved. 'Miss Look for the

Positive!'

'Exactly. Except I expect you to refer to me as 'Missus,' if you please!'

It was hard to leave Skye, even though they knew they would return one day. Their honeymoon had been wonderful, thought Cass, but there was excitement, too, in knowing that they would be going back to their own home and starting life as a married couple.

There was one more week before term began, although Cass had a substantial pile of paperwork to tackle first. She hadn't found time to start it before the wedding, so was glad that they quickly turned her 'cubbyhole' into a serviceable study. Autumn was always a busy term, with new children settling in, and the momentum increasing after half-term as everyone prepared for Christmas.

Matt spent most days at his headquarters, doing essential groundwork before the latest project could begin. He and Cass didn't discuss his decision to return to African waters, and she felt immeasurably relieved that they'd been honest with each other. The only way this marriage could work was for Matt to know she was happy, despite his regular absences. There was no certain outcome to this voyage they were undertaking, but — she smiled as the cliché came to mind — there looked to be a fair wind ahead.

At the start of term, Cass left home each morning, and found on her return that Matt had either prepared dinner or made plans to go to a nearby bistro that had become their favourite eating place.

On the fifth morning, Friday, he was ready to leave immediately after breakfast. He'd packed the previous evening, and Cass tried to quell the sinking feeling in her stomach as she saw his suitcase, still unfastened, on the bedroom floor. Deliberately, she didn't linger over their goodbyes, pretending that she had to be at school extra early today. Whether he believed it or not, she didn't know. He raised an eyebrow but didn't try to delay her.

At the end of the day, she returned home and opened the front door.

Emptiness hung about the apartment and echoed in her ears. Having been with Matt almost all day and night for several weeks, it was hard to go back to the old ways — dinner on a tray in front of the television, finding only dry towels, no wet floor, in the bathroom. Worst of all, there was an empty space the size of a shopping mall on his side of the bed.

Saturday dawned. Cass opened her eyes. And then she remembered. She stretched out a hand and touched the pillow where Matt's head would have lain. Then, with no more hesitation, she jumped up, had a shower, and rang Judy, an old school friend who belonged to the tennis club. By mid-morning they were playing a game of singles, which became a doubles match when they were joined by two other players.

Some of the staff had been invited for a working supper to discuss the school's overseas exchange programme. A dozen children from Italy were due to arrive on Monday, having been corresponding with others here whose families would welcome the Italians into their homes and entertain them.

On Tuesday, Lyn stopped Cass in the corridor. 'Can we meet at lunchtime? I've a proposition for you. You can say no, but I hope you won't.' As an afterthought, she called over her shoulder, 'Bring us something to eat, will you?'

Intrigued, Cass turned up at the end of the morning with sandwiches and coffees.

'Can you face taking a dozen of our kids to Italy next week?' As Cass blinked, Lyn went on, 'Not on your own, of course. It's just that Mo Fletcher and Bill Jones were due to escort them. But Mo rang to say her daughter's been hospitalised with a particularly bad bout of asthma. Even if the girl's discharged quite quickly, I can't expect Mo to leave her and buzz off to Europe. So I wondered if you would go instead?'

Cass didn't hesitate. It would be a responsibility, but an experience she would enjoy. Bill Jones was popular, but most of all capable, so all should be well.

The journey to Rome went smoothly,

and the children were greeted by their various pen-friends. Cass and Bill met all the parents and, reassured, sent their slightly nervous London charges off to absorb Italian culture. The visit should improve their language skills, but it wouldn't do to place a bet on it! Cass loved revisiting Rome, which she had first seen as a teenager; and the small hotel was conveniently situated, so she and Bill were free to wander. All the children from England carried mobile phones, so contact wasn't a problem, but hopefully there wouldn't be any hitches.

Although Matt was always at the back of her mind and in her heart, she didn't worry about him. They managed a brief conversation when he rang her hotel one evening. Everything was going well on the *Venus,* and he was delighted to know that Cass was enjoying herself.

She had hardly reached home again when her friend, Marion, telephoned. She asked Cass about the trip, but then in her forthright way said she'd actually rung about the animal ambulance. Could

Cass help out this weekend? Not in the charity shop, but as a driver. One of their patients, an injured woodpecker, was ready to return to the parkland where he'd been found. His wing had healed and, said Marion, he was demanding discharge! Cass had driven the animal ambulance, a small van, previously, and agreed to deliver him home.

On Saturday, she stood in woodland a few miles from central London. The sun was filtering through the leaves, a network of delicate green lace. When she opened the cage door, the bird seemed to heave a sigh of relief, and then, without a word of thanks, spread his wings and flew away.

As she started the engine, ready to leave, Cass found herself laughing. Tonight she was due to have dinner with her father and Liz. Tomorrow she was scheduled to play in a tennis match, and then tomorrow evening she must prepare Monday's lessons. Somehow she must find time for housework.

There was a lot to do before Matt came home.

Other titles in the
Linford Romance Library:

SUMMER'S DREAM

Jean M. Long

Talented designer Juliet Croft is devastated when the company she works for closes. She takes a temporary job at the Linden Manor Hotel, but soon hears rumours that the business is in financial difficulties — and suspects that Sheldon's, a rival company, is involved. During her work, she renews her friendship with Scott, a former colleague. At the same time, she must cope with her growing feelings for Martin Glover, the hotel manager. Trouble is, he's already taken . . .

SEEING SHADOWS

Susan Udy

Lexie Brookes is busy running her hairdressing salon and wondering what to do about her cooling relationship with her partner, Danny. When the jewellery shop next door is broken into via her own premises, the owner — the wealthy and infuriatingly arrogant Bruno Cavendish — blames her for his losses. Then Danny disappears, and Lexie is suddenly targeted by a mysterious stalker. To add to the turmoil, Bruno appears to be attracted to her, and she finds herself equally drawn to him . . .

A DATE WITH ROMANCE

Toni Anders

Refusing to live in the shadow of her father, a famous TV chef, Lauren Tate runs her own cake shop with her best friend, Daisy. Having been unlucky in love, Lauren pours her energy into her business — until she meets her handsome new neighbour, Jake, who is keen to strike up a friendship with her. Will Lauren decide to take him up on the offer? Then Daisy has an accident, and announces she'll be following her partner to America once she has healed — leaving Lauren with some difficult choices . . .